MURDER GRINS AND BEARS IT

This Large Print Book carries the
Seal of Approval of N.A.V.H.

MURDER GRINS AND BEARS IT

DEB BAKER

WHEELER PUBLISHING
An imprint of Thomson Gale, a part of The Thomson Corporation

Detroit • New York • San Francisco • New Haven, Conn. • Waterville, Maine • London

LIBRARY OF CONGRESS CATALOGING-IN-PUBLICATION DATA

Baker, Deb, 1953–
    Murder grins and bears it / by Deb Baker. — Large print ed.
        p. cm. — (Wheeler Publishing large print cozy mystery)
    "A Yooper mystery" — T.p. verso.
    ISBN-13: 978-1-59722-615-8 (pbk. : alk. paper)
    ISBN-10: 1-59722-615-7 (pbk. : alk. paper)
    1. Upper Peninsula (Mich.) — Fiction. 2. Grandmothers — Fiction.
3. Women private investigators — Fiction. 4. Bear hunting — Fiction.
5. Large type books. I. Title.
PS3602.A586M85 2007b
813'.6—dc22   2007023230

Published in 2007 by arrangement with Midnight Ink,
an imprint of Llewellyn Publications.

Printed in the United States of America on permanent paper
10 9 8 7 6 5 4 3 2 1

To Red McGarity, Tim McGarity, and Ed Maleszewski, who captivated my imagination with tales, tall and otherwise.

ONE

I wasn't surprised when they hauled the first human body out of the back woods on Monday, day three of the season.

That's bear hunting season, and although it starts in September in the Michigan Upper Peninsula, hunters were scampering around in the woods long before that, setting bait piles and hoping for one good illegal shot. Once they had the official go-ahead to start blasting, nothing could hold them back.

As usual I wasn't around when the body was discovered in midmorning. Remembering back, I think I heard the shot first thing this morning.

I missed the action because I was busy stealing my grandson's car. His white Ford Escort had a stick shift and an extra pedal on the floor, which threw me for a loop since I've only been driving a few months and had been teaching myself on a vehicle

7

with an automatic transmission. But my behind-the-wheel practice had been on hold ever since I totaled my truck.

My best friend, Cora Mae, was sitting in the passenger seat of the Escort while I tried to keep it running, but it hopped around the yard like a jackrabbit. That's when I heard the shot. At the time, though, I thought it was the car backfiring or maybe the gears grinding.

My name is Gertie Johnson and I'm a recent widow. Cora Mae says I shouldn't tell people that, because two years have passed since Barney died, but I say I'll stop when I'm good and ready. Cora Mae says sixty-six years old is too young to lose interest in life. She's the expert since she's buried three husbands.

I have to admit, the police scanner she gave me last year sure helped put the pink back in my cheeks.

Listening to my scanner is better than watching soap operas because it's real life and I know most of the names coming across the air waves. I'm right in the thick of things, where I like to be, and that's why I was stealing the car.

It's all part of my plans for my new detective business.

Little Donny, my Milwaukee grandson,

arrived late last night clutching the bear hunting license he'd won in the Michigan bear lottery. He was driving his old Ford Escort with a bad muffler, so he woke up everybody in Stonely coming into town, including me.

Before Cora Mae came over, Carl Anderson showed up at my house bright and early for a quick cup of coffee. He was headed into the woods to hunt.

I needed transportation today, so I formulated my travel plans right on the spot.

Though it would appear simple to have Little Donny drive me, I learned the hard way that life is easier when family members aren't involved in every little thing I do. They tend to accidentally botch my plans or they misunderstand my intentions and get all bent out of shape trying to stop me.

Like the time Blaze thought I'd lost my savings and tried to prove in a court of law that I was incompetent to manage my own affairs. He came out of that one looking really bad. Or the time Little Donny blew my cover when I was on a surveillance mission. It just doesn't pay to confide in family.

Things would have been simpler still if I hadn't totaled the truck Barney left me or if Cora Mae would take up driving. I'm sick and tired of begging rides and explaining my business to everyone, especially Blaze, my interfering son, who also happens to be the local sheriff.

Blaze and I have always butted heads. I'm a go-getter and he's a sit-downer, and that bothers him more than it does me. Plus, he still gets worked up about his name. His sisters, Heather and Star, don't mind being named for the horses I never had. They think it's cute and so do I.

For some reason Blaze doesn't agree.

I started a fresh pot of coffee and had Carl help me haul Little Donny out of bed, which isn't the easiest thing in the world, considering Little Donny must weigh a good two hundred and eighty pounds and hauling is really what we had to do. A beached whale would have been easier to tackle.

It's a good thing Carl is big and burly, but most of the Swedes around here are. On the other hand, I'm about five foot two, or used to be before I started getting old. But I'm stronger than I look.

Nineteen-year-olds are like growing babies, testing the world and making all kinds of mistakes. And Little Donny would sleep till noon if I let him. Last night he could hardly wait for morning to get into the woods and do some hunting. This morning, all he cared about was whatever dream put that silly smile on his face right before we woke him up.

After Carl and I prodded and poked him, he opened one eye, held his arm up to check the time on his watch, and groaned. "It's only five thirty, Granny. Leave me alone."

"You're in Michigan now, not Milwaukee," I reminded him. "It's six thirty here and half the day's gone." I pulled the pillow out from under him. His head bounced a few times, then he flipped onto his right side and closed his eyes.

When I realized he wasn't going to co-operate, I dug under the covers at the foot of the bed and hauled one beefy leg over the side. Carl helped me finish rolling him out. We dragged him to the kitchen table in his boxer underwear with the pictures of footballs on them and started pumping coffee into him.

Little Donny and Carl had done some deer hunting together last fall, and even though Carl's closer to my age than my grandson's, they became fast friends. They stayed friends even after Little Donny loaded a buck into Carl's brand new station wagon and then discovered it wasn't dead. The inside of Carl's wagon was shredded like coleslaw by the time he got the buck out, and Little Donny didn't look so good either.

But Carl didn't hold it against Little Donny. It takes a lot to ruffle Carl's feathers. Which reminded me of chicken fat.

I took a two-pound coffee can from the refrigerator and placed it on the table. "Here's the can of chicken grease you wanted," I said.

Carl opened the lid and poked the congealed chicken fat with one finger. "It's hard as a rock," he said. "Why'd you store it in the fridge?" He handed it back. "Put it on the stove burner for a few minutes to soften it up, but don't let it get too hot. Don't want to burn myself."

I fired up the gas and moved the can to the burner.

"I'm finally gonna get my bear this year, Gertie." Carl poured more coffee and leaned back so the front legs of the chair were off the floor, which drives me crazy. Teetering like that was nothing but a fall waiting to happen, and it had happened plenty over the years. You'd think they'd learn.

"Bears love chickens," he continued. "I know that because every time they've raided my garbage, it's right after we had chicken

12

for supper and had throwed away the bones."

"They sure do love chicken," I agreed. "They love pigs, too. Remember the time Old Ben tried to raise pigs?"

Carl laughed so hard he began to snort.

Old Ben had bought six little piglets in Escanaba, and before the end of the month none were left. Pigs and chickens are considered bear snacks and don't last long in the Upper Peninsula, or the U.P. as we call it.

Little Donny had one eye open after his first cup of coffee. I poured him another.

"There's an orange shirt in the closet for you," I said. "Go put it on."

Little Donny grumbled off to the bedroom, clutching his coffee cup, his hair standing up straight on one side of his head like he'd ironed it that way.

"Lick your hair down while you're at it," I called after him. "And hurry." I had to get him out of my way before I could put my plan in motion.

"Gonna smear that chicken grease all over myself." Carl had a smug look on his face like he was Einstein discussing an important new relativity theory. "That way when I move around from bait pile to bait pile they'll pick up my scent and follow me right over. Don't tell nobody. It's my secret ingredient."

That's got to be the dumbest idea Carl's had in a long time, but I didn't say so. The Finns and Swedes are dominant in this part of the U.P., and after you live with them for a while you notice they're a proud bunch. You don't call them dumb right to their faces. You wait until they actually do the dumb thing, then you tell everybody in town and they help you rub it in forever.

Carl's as Swedish as it gets, so he's done his own share of teasing.

Instead I tried to direct him away from his dumb strategy. "I think there's some bear magnet spray that Barney used to use. You can spray some of that on the ground. Barney swore by it."

Carl shook his head. "I tried that spray and it didn't work. This is my own special formula, and once I prove how good it works, I'm gonna sell it out of the trunk of my car next year and get rich. Just you wait and see."

"Hope you've got your rifle scope sighted in," I said. "You don't want to miss when that bear hurtles at you, because you get only one shot. Miss and you're bear lunch."

Carl rose from the table, stirred the chicken grease with a spoon, and turned off

14

the burner. "I'm bow and arrow hunting. Got myself some new arrows, ends are sharp like razor blades."

I gaped in astonishment. Anyone who smears chicken grease all over himself and goes bear hunting with a bow and arrow is plain stupid or has a death wish.

During gun season for bears there's no law against bow and arrow hunting like there is during deer hunting season, but there should be. Whoever made up the bear rules must have been pounding back shots of brandy while he wrote them. Besides, bow and arrow hunters are exempt from the hunter orange rule, and they run around out in the brush in camouflage. Even though there isn't as much traffic in the woods as during deer season, I think it's always risky to be out in camo with rifles going off.

Carl had a lot going against him. If he survived the bear mistaking him for lunch, someone with a firearm would finish him off. The best thing that could have happened to Carl would have been losing the bear lottery in June.

"Why don't you wait till archery season to play with your bow and arrow?"

"That's three weeks away. All the bears will be shot up by then."

"Better take Little Donny along with his

rifle for backup," I suggested, implementing my plan to get Little Donny out of the way.

"Sure. He already knows that I get first shot with my arrow. If I miss, then he gets a go-around."

Little Donny shuffled out of the bedroom wearing the orange shirt I'd bought for him on sale in Escanaba. I'd bought the same for myself plus a pair of orange suspender pants and a new pair of running shoes. Not that I run anywhere these days. They're just comfortable, and they put a little forward spring in my step.

Although a lot of women in this part of the country hunt, I don't, but I still need orange clothes for traipsing around in the woods. Those hunters shoot at anything that moves.

"You don't have time for breakfast," I said to Little Donny when he opened the refrigerator door and bent down to peer inside.

"I have about thirty pounds of day-old bakery in the car," Carl told him. "Bear bait. You can eat some of that."

Little Donny perked right up, plopped Barney's old orange cap with Budweiser printed across the front on his head, and followed Carl and his coffee can of chicken grease out the door.

"Stay away from Carl's can of chicken

16

grease," I called out to Little Donny. I didn't want my favorite grandson smelling like a chicken and getting mauled by a ravenous bear that weighed three times what he did.

About time, I thought when they pulled out of the driveway in Carl's station wagon. I rushed through the house, grabbing my Blublocker sunglasses and oversized purse from the dresser. After rummaging through Little Donny's suitcase and clothes, I pulled his car keys out of his jacket, which lay in a heap on the floor next to his bed. I let out a loud sigh of relief. If the keys had been in the pants he was wearing, I'd have been dead in the water.

At seven thirty I tried to start Little Donny's car. I worked on it for fifteen minutes before phoning Cora Mae, who lives down the road.

"If I remember right," I said to her, "one of your husbands used to drive a stick shift car."

"That was Earl," Cora Mae said, chewing something crunchy into the phone.

"By any chance, did you pay attention to how he did it?"

"Did what?" Cora Mae is a mite slow in the morning but by noon she's sharp as a cracked bullwhip.

17

"Did you pay attention to how he made the car go?"

"Oh sure. He tried to teach me, but I couldn't get the hang of it. Your feet and hands have to work at the same time. It's complicated."

"But do you remember how he did it?"

"Sort of."

"I need your help," I said. "Come right over."

I waited outside impatiently until she eventually strolled up the driveway in her black, sleeveless knit top, black stretch pants, and high-heeled black sandals. Cora Mae just turned sixty-three but she doesn't look or act her age. The knit top was low cut and as tight as a sausage casing. Cora Mae discovered Wonderbras last year and hasn't been out of them since. Her boobs stand right up and lead the way.

"Cora Mae, can you speed it up a little?" I said. "I'm going to miss the auction."

She sashayed into the passenger seat and studied the stick shift. "That's a clutch," she said, pointing at the extra foot pedal. "You have to synchronize it with the gas." She used her hands to demonstrate. "Give it a try."

She remembered most of it. The only part she got wrong was the shifting order. After I tried to start out in fourth gear a few times and did the jackrabbit hop, she remembered it right, and we took off down the drive.

We blasted out onto the road in the stolen Ford Escort at the same time as we heard the bang.

"What was that?" Cora Mae wanted to know.

"This piece of junk is backfiring," I said, grinding through the gears. "And Little Donny needs a new muffler."

The county auction is held annually at the Escanaba fairgrounds, forty miles down the road from Stonely. All the surrounding municipalities get together and sell stuff they don't need anymore. Last year when I still had Barney's truck, I drove over and paid only thirty dollars for a perfectly good power saw the forestry department was auctioning off.

"Where are you getting the money from to bid on a truck?" Cora Mae asked on the way over. "I thought you were trying to live on your Social Security."

"I've got resources," I hedged.

"You dug up your money box, didn't you?"

"It's for a good cause."

After Barney died, I went to the bank and

withdrew every last penny of our money and buried it in a waterproof steel box under the apple tree. It's my insurance against failing banks and an untrustworthy government.

I had to put it all back in the bank to beat Blaze in court, but that was only a temporary arrangement.

My purse was stuffed with wadded greenbacks, but I intended to hang on to as many as possible.

I dropped Cora Mae and her high heels at the main gate and parked Little Donny's Escort on the side of the road about three blocks from the fairgrounds, hoping nobody would park close by. If I had to use reverse, I was in real trouble.

We were just in time for the automotive part of the auction, and Blaze's old sheriff's truck was the first vehicle on the block.

"Now, I know this truck don't look like much," the auctioneer hollered while the crowd hooted and roared with laughter, "but it sure can run. Only a hundred thousand miles on it, and a hundred left to go."

You could hardly hear him over the howling going on.

"What happened to it?" yelled a fat heckler with a skull and crossbones tattooed on his arm. "Looks like some clown spray-painted it yellow. Look, they even spray-painted the door handle and all the trim."

The crowd roared. I was beginning to get annoyed, especially after the clown remark. I took it personally since I was the one who'd tried to snazzy up Blaze's rust bucket with a little new paint. I did it to help him out and never got a thank you for it.

In hindsight, I do have to admit spray paint isn't the best way to touch up a paint job. The paint ran in streaks in some spots and it was real hard to keep off the windows. That's why I went ahead and sprayed the trim. Paint was on the chrome already anyway.

"Better haul this one off to the junkyard," some other wit in the crowd shouted.

I kept my eyes on the truck. It still had the lights and siren on the roof and I was going to need that. Someone had peeled off the Sheriff's Department lettering but I could still read what it had said since it was a different shade of yellow from the rest of the truck.

"Five hundred dollars," I called out.

The auctioneer's head swung in my direction. "We're starting the bidding out at eight hundred. That's rock bottom."

"Then I'm bidding rock bottom," I said.

Rock bottom went once, twice, three

times. Sold to the little red-haired lady in the orange suspender pants.

That was me, although my hair is more a light copper shade than actual red.

I grinned to beat the band.

"How are we going to get both your new truck and Little Donny's car home?" Cora Mae wanted to know.

"That's why I brought you along," I said. "The truck is an automatic. You'll be able to drive it. I'll drive Little Donny's car with the stick shift and you can follow me in the truck."

"But I never renewed my driver's license. I don't have one."

"Neither do I, but in case you haven't noticed, I drive just fine." Which was sort of a lie. I've had a few scary moments and I've done a little damage, mostly to my own property. My first attempt at driving was in Barney's old truck, and I only drove it for a week before I rolled it into a ditch. "There's no other way to do it, Cora Mae. You have to."

I paid up, filled out the required forms, and motioned Cora Mae to hop into the passenger seat of my new truck. I drove it out the side gate of the fairgrounds, around the block, and parked next to Little Donny's car. I pulled a screwdriver from the back seat of the Escort and screwed Barney's old truck plates onto my bright yellow truck.

After taking all this in without lifting a manicured finger to help, Cora Mae slid into the driver's seat of my new business vehicle and waited to follow me in the Ford Escort. My grandson's car jumped and lurched onto the road. I ground the gears, the engine roared, I popped the clutch, and the car tore off.

I was going to have whiplash before I got this piece of junk back to Little Donny.

Before leaving Escanaba, I turned into the parking lot at the hardware store, with Cora Mae trailing in the yellow truck.

"I'll be right back," I yelled to her and hitched my heavy purse up on my shoulder.

The purse hung as heavy as a bucketful of well water, but it was a critical part of my summer wardrobe. It's a lot easier to stash concealed weapons in the wintertime than in the summer. In the winter, I wear a fishing vest under my hunting jacket and fill all those little pockets with everything I need. I don't have that choice when hot weather rolls around.

Moments later I came out of the hardware store carrying a lettering kit with sheets of black letters in different sizes.

"Let's hit it," I called to Cora Mae.

I saw the commotion as soon as I turned down Old Peterson Road. Cora Mae, following behind, almost hit me when I slowed suddenly. Sheriff and fire vehicles jammed the road, all trying to one-up each other by running every strobe light they had. An ambulance, off to the side of the road, was surrounded by deputies. One lane was sectioned off and guarded by a group of men I recognized as assistant deputy volunteers. Blaze had recruited them when he was reelected last year.

Word in the U.P. travels faster than a skunked dog races for home. About thirty spectators had gathered — not much of a crowd yet, which meant this was fresh-breaking news.

I pulled over, careful to leave room between Little Donny's Ford Escort and the next vehicle so I could get out. Cora Mae parked behind me. I ran back to my new truck, opened the driver's door and reached past Cora Mae to flip the lights and siren switches. Might as well join the action. If I looked official I might be able to drive right into the middle of the commotion.

Nothing happened. I flipped the switches

three more times before I gave up. "Dang," I muttered. "Nothing ever works when you need it."

Cora Mae teetered behind me in her spiked heels as I elbowed my way to the front of the group.

"Gertie Johnson," I said, identifying myself to the volunteer deputy facing me. "I have clearance to move through."

"I'm sorry, but I have orders from Blaze and he says everyone stays on that side of the line." He stretched his arms out along the rope.

"I'm the sheriff's mother, do you know that?" He didn't flinch when I tried to intimidate him with my most threatening expression.

"Yes, ma'am, I know, but Blaze said nobody can pass. He didn't leave special instructions for you."

Time to switch tactics. "What happened here?" I asked him sweetly. I scanned the crowd of officials, looking for Blaze. The volunteer, busy holding his line, didn't respond, so I turned back to the crowd. "Does anybody know what's going on?"

"Don't know," a man next to me said. He pointed off in the direction of the woods. "They carried someone out on a stretcher a little while ago. I'm guessing it was a dead

25

body considerin' the way it was covered up head to toe with a blanket, eh."

"Dead hunter, for sure," someone said.

"Car accident," a woman offered.

"No crashed car around here," someone else said. "It's a dead hunter."

Something inside of me wanted to scream. I grabbed Cora Mae by the arm and squeezed. "Little Donny and Carl were hunting back in there," I croaked, not bothering to hide the panic in my voice. "Where's my grandson?"

"Don't even think it, Gertie. They're okay."

"Little Donny was hunting back there," I repeated, feeling flushed and dizzy.

TWO

Recovering slightly, I ducked under the rope and broke into a lope in my brand-new running shoes. I wasn't thinking too clearly. Fear wound a knot in my stomach and I felt a surge of adrenaline. I planned to run as long as it took to find my grandson.

A firm grip on the back of my suspenders snapped me back.

"Where you going, Ma?" a familiar voice said.

"Let go of me," I cried before I realized it was my son, Blaze.

He released his hold, and I grabbed his arm and clenched it. "Where is he?" I demanded.

"Where's who?" Blaze's face was pale.

"I heard someone's dead," I said, squeezing his arm tighter. "Little Donny was in the woods with Carl. Where's Little Donny? Where's Carl?"

Time seemed to crawl. Blaze opened his

mouth and very slowly the words traveled through the air. I was about to smack him I was so desperate to hear reassuring words.

"Carl's over by my truck," Blaze said, pointing in the direction of the ambulance, "and Little Donny seems to be missing at the moment."

"Little Donny's not in the ambulance, is he? Please tell me he isn't in the ambulance."

"No, Ma. He's not."

I released my grip on Blaze's arm and clutched at my pounding heart. "That's a relief. For a minute there, I had a very bad feeling. I need to sit down."

Blaze motioned and a folding camp chair appeared out of nowhere. I dropped into it and steadied my nerves.

"Who's in the ambulance?"

"A guy named Robert Hendricks."

I searched my memory. "I don't know any Robert Hendricks. Where's he from?"

"He worked with the Department of Natural Resources out of Marquette. That's why you don't know him. A DNR agent."

The DNR and its agents aren't viewed as assets to our local communities. Slinking around in the underbrush like Brown Recluse spiders and spying on the very people who pay their wages doesn't make them

28

popular.

"Murder?" I said.

"No doubt about it. It must have happened this morning."

I remembered the sound I'd heard earlier. I'd assumed it was Little Donny's car, but it could have been a rifle shot.

"I heard the shot," I informed Blaze.

"What makes you think that?"

"I was out in the yard about eight and I heard something."

Blaze scribbled in his notebook and flipped it closed. "I'll look into it."

His beer belly poured over the top of his belt, which was riding dangerously low on his hips, and a button had popped off his uniform shirt from the force of the swell.

I stood up. "I think I'll stick around and talk to Carl. Where do you think Little Donny went?"

"Ma, don't worry. I'm sure Little Donny's fine. Go on home." He had me by the elbow, dismissing me in his usual manner with a personal escort out of the circle of action. "Where's your partner in crime?"

"Here I am," Cora Mae called from the spectator side of the rope. "Over this way."

Just then the ambulance started up and edged toward the road.

"I want to get a look at the body before

29

they drive away," I said, pulling on my arm. "Get your hands off me and stop that vehicle. I have to see with my own eyes that it isn't Donny."

"Nothing doing. I told you it isn't him."

The ambulance moved past and the volunteers forced the crowd to the side of the road. Blaze held on to me with an iron grip.

"Where's that ambulance going? Escanaba or Marquette?" I demanded.

Blaze let go when he was sure the ambulance was clear. "The Escanaba morgue," he said.

I knew I could follow the ambulance the forty minutes it would take to drive to the Escanaba morgue, but that sour lemon who ran the morgue wouldn't let me look at the body anyway.

I sighed as the ambulance streaked down the road, kicking gravel and dust into a cloud behind it.

The volunteer deputies encouraged everyone to disperse, and most, seeing the ambulance pull away with the corpse, moved toward their vehicles.

I thought I should move my new truck before Blaze saw it because this wasn't the time or the place to explain my new purchase. But Blaze was scrawling in his notebook, which he perched on his swollen belly. He wasn't paying attention to the crowd or the parked vehicles. Someone from the mass of law-enforcement officials called his name and he walked away.

I stood watching Blaze's back as he lumbered off. I glanced at the woods where the man in the crowd had pointed to show me the direction they had carried the body from. Towering grasses lined the road against a backdrop of tall pine trees, and a deer trail meandered into the canopy and curved out of sight.

Glancing back, I caught a glimpse of Carl in the group of deputies. I'd give my uppers to hear what they were saying.

I put on my thinking cap. "They hauled that body out of Carl's bait pile," I said to Cora Mae. "If Carl wasn't involved somehow, he'd still be hiding in a tree overlooking his pile of bakery, waiting for a black bear to wander through. He wouldn't even know about the shooting."

This stretch of woods is called Bear Pass by the locals because bears like to follow an established circuit, looping around and covering the same territory over again. The idea is to plant your stand right where they come through. Because Carl's bait pile was in a prime spot on Bear Pass, he should have been staked out.

Instead, Carl stood smack-dab in the middle of the action.

Cora Mae wasn't paying much attention to me, focusing instead on one of the volunteers. I saw her give him a tiny wave, a flutter of fingers at waist level, which produced a weak grin from him.

"Let's move 'em out," a volunteer deputy yelled to the stragglers like a cowboy rounding up a herd of cattle. "You too, ladies." He motioned to us.

We walked down the road toward our vehicles. When we got to Little Donny's car, I opened the driver's door and bent in to retrieve my oversized purse. Then I straightened up, closed the door, and surveyed the situation.

"Follow my lead," I whispered to Cora Mae. "Get ready."

I watched the inevitable traffic jam form on the road as spectators tried to pull their trucks out and swing around all at the same time. I waited for the perfect moment, then ran across the road and popped into the woods. I couldn't help noticing that Cora Mae wasn't behind me.

I peered out of the tree line and saw her standing in the middle of the road looking like she'd lost her way.

"Psst," I hissed. "Pssst." Louder.

Finally she noticed me and dodged around a red pickup with a swarm of kids riding in the open bed of the truck.

"Once in a while," Cora Mae crabbed when she caught up, "you ought to tell me what's going on ahead of time."

"I'm improvising as I go," I explained. "You just have to pay better attention."

I've lived in the Michigan woods for forty-some years and I like to think I know my way around them the same way I know every liver spot on the back of my hand. Yoopers, as those of us living in the Upper Peninsula are called by the rest of the country, have a reputation for an innate sense of direction.

We don't need compasses.

I glanced up at the sky showing through the treetops, noted the position of the sun so we wouldn't get lost, and set out at a fair clip, considering Cora Mae was wearing high heels and I wasn't a young goose anymore.

September is the perfect time of year for a woods walk. The mosquitoes are tapering off, so you still have some blood in your body when you come out of the forest, and the ticks are gone. The gooseberries have turned from green to purple and a few maple leaves have just started to turn. The only sound is the buzz of bees hurrying to finish their business, and in our case, the sound of Pocahontas crashing through the woods behind me.

I looked back and noticed scratches on Cora Mae's face.

"Did you fall down?" I asked.

"Why would you think that?"

"You have burrs stuck all over in your hair."

Burdock is the nastiest weed I've ever come across and I'm determined to snuff it off the face of the earth. The Indians used to boil the roots and eat them, but I tried it and it's not worth the effort. In late summer it puts out seed in burrs, which stick to everything like Velcro. Nasty stuff.

Cora Mae was beginning to drag. "How much farther?" She sounded like a ten-year-old on a road trip.

I frowned. "We should have hit Bear Pass by now. Maybe it's just ahead. Let's keep going."

"How are we going to know when we're there?"

"The trail widens out. You'll see. Trust me."

We heard a rifle shot go off.

"That seemed awfully close," Cora Mae said.

Another shot went off.

"Sound travels a long way in the woods," I said, trying to convince myself. The gunfire *did* sound near.

"I have to sit down for a minute." She wandered over to a fallen tree and plunked down.

"How are you ever going to be a Trouble Buster with shoes like that?" I lectured. Trouble Busters was our official business name since we discovered there are all kinds of rules before you can call yourself a private investigator. And after careful consideration and a lot of noise and threats from Blaze, we decided we didn't qualify. Hence, the cover name, Trouble Busters.

I continued to complain. "You can't walk. You can't sneak up on anybody. You can't do any of the things you need to do to be an investigator."

"This wasn't my business idea, remember? We haven't had a single case. We haven't made a single cent."

Well, it was true the brainstorm to start the investigator — I mean buster — business was mine, and it was also true we hadn't had work yet, but all that was about to change.

"Now that we have a truck we can start advertising."

"And who's going to hire us?"

"Lots of people."

"This isn't TV, you know. Besides, Blaze already told you it's illegal to call yourself an investigator unless you have a license, and last I checked, neither of us comes close to qualifying."

"That's exactly why we are using Trouble Busters."

I thought I heard Cora Mae mutter "stupid name" under her breath, but I could have imagined it.

I used the rest stop as an opportunity to drop my purse and rub my shoulder.

I bought the biggest purse I could find. Besides the regular stuff you'd carry in one, I've got pepper spray, a stun gun, and handcuffs, which I didn't think I needed until Cora Mae bought a pair and actually got a chance to use them last year to restrain a criminal. The stun gun was borrowed from my friend George, and I liked it so much I told him I lost it.

Cora Mae looked off ahead. She pointed. "And you," she said, "can't find your way around your own backyard."

I looked where she pointed, following her lacquered index finger. Through a break in the trees, I could see a road. Bending down, I could make out my new yellow truck.

We had walked in a circle. So much for the dependability of the sun.

After studying the situation for a moment, I said, "I think I know where we went wrong. Let's go."

"The only place I'm going is home to my easy chair," Cora Mae informed me, pulling off a shoe and massaging her foot. "I've had it."

"We have to check out the crime scene before the FBI shows up and ships all the evidence to Washington and covers up the crime." Granted, I was a little overdramatic, but Cora Mae loves drama, and it stood to reason that the FBI would get involved, considering a government employee was murdered.

She frowned.

"I just want to study the crime scene for future reference," I said. "Come on. We could use the practice, and I'm really concerned about Little Donny."

"I've had it," Cora Mae repeated.

"Fine by me. Take the truck when you go before Blaze sees it. I'm not in the mood to explain it to him."

I watched her teeter out onto Old Peterson Road and crawl into my new truck.

■ ■ ■ ■

I passed a wild apple tree and picked a small green apple. I've always loved to eat apples before they're ripe. A little salt and an unripe, sour apple is the best thing in the world. I nibbled cautiously around a wormhole. My deceased husband, Barney, used to say that the hole means the worm came out of the apple, not because it went in, but I've always had my doubts.

I'm not taking any chances.

It sounds crazy, but I felt Barney's spirit by my side. I loved that man more than anything in the world and thought I'd die when I heard he was gone.

I couldn't think of a reason to go on.

After enough time passed, I realized that my kids were worth living for, but I still had to find something fascinating enough to make me want to get out of bed every day.

My new investigation business had accomplished that.

Just as I was thinking I was good and lost, I spotted yellow crime scene tape ahead. Cinnamon rolls, doughnuts, and bread were dumped in the middle of a clearing, and I saw my coffee can filled with gelled chicken grease next to a large oak tree.

I rummaged in my everything-but-the-kitchen-sink purse and located a pair of binoculars. Careful to stay well on my side of the tape, I scanned the murder site. In the center of the clearing I saw a dark, wet spot about the size of a double bed where blood must have seeped into the ground.

By zooming in through the lenses of my binoculars, I could make out large footprints planted smack in the center of the wet area. Little Donny's rifle, given to him by his grandfather, lay on the ground, not more than three feet from the wet spot.

I saw what I thought might be bits of brain and bone, but I might have imagined it since I've never actually seen those things.

Peering up into the trees, I spotted Carl's tree stand. It appeared to be the size of a postage stamp, which left me wondering where Little Donny had staked out. Little Donny, also known in the family circle as Beefy Boy, couldn't have shinnied up that tree if the mother of all bears was on his behind.

Scrutinizing the perimeter of the clearing, I noticed broken branches off to the left of the tree stand. Behind some brush, I found Little Donny's hideout. I could tell by the matted ground covering and the doughnut crumbs.

The scene must have been exactly the same as it was when the murder occurred. Except for the body. Any minute now, crime specialists would descend, like turkey vultures, and pick the area clean.

I certainly didn't want to be found snooping around.

After one last sweep with the binoculars and noticing nothing new, I walked in a wide loop around the back of the yellow tape and noticed something I'd missed before. And it wasn't inside the taped area.

Behind the bait pile on the opposite side of the trail the brush was flattened like a herd of deer had bedded down in it. That's what I thought it was at first, but then I noticed a faint indentation like a tire mark, a patterned tire crease at the front of the brush and more at the back. Someone had driven a vehicle right through the brush.

Puzzling over the significance of my find, I kicked through the brush and a flash of red caught my eye. Picking the object up, I rolled it in my palm. It was a very large tooth, a very large, red tooth, larger than a wisdom tooth, and redder than . . . well, redder than any tooth I ever saw before. Not sure what to do with it, I put it in my pocket.

I scanned the scene one last time, still very concerned for my grandson. Little Donny was probably at my house right this minute, eating his way through the refrigerator and wondering where his car was. Wishful thinking, I know, but there wasn't anything more to do here. Time to go home.

Earlier, when Cora Mae and I first pulled over to check out the commotion, I thought every sheriff and deputy in the Upper Peninsula must be standing around watching the action. I was wrong. There were even more cops now than before.

There were more law enforcement officials swarming around than flies on horse pies on a hot summer day, all of them focused on Little Donny's Ford Escort. I've never seen so many uniforms.

Blaze stood off from the car talking to a large muscular man with a buzz cut who was wearing a brown uniform and a side-arm. His face was as square as a wood block. I walked up behind Blaze and tapped him on the shoulder. Mr. Always-Be-Prepared almost jumped out of his shorts.

"What's going on?" I asked.

"Geez, Ma, where'd you come from?" Blaze frowned and bent over to pick up the pen he had dropped when I startled him. I could see his butt crack. His wife Mary better put him on a diet, pronto.

"I missed my ride home. What's going on?" I repeated, pointing at Little Donny's car.

"I was just explaining the circumstances to Warden Burnett."

"Nice to meet you," I said, extending a hand which buzz cut proceeded to crush. "I'm the sheriff's mother."

"I'm the Marquette D-DNR district supervisor," he said to me, then turned his attention back to Blaze. "I c-couldn't get here s-sooner. I was out in the field."

Either I had an acute hearing problem or the warden had a bit of a stutter.

"As I was explaining to Warden Burnett, this car seems to have appeared out of nowhere." Blaze scratched his head, a motion designed to facilitate thinking, but it wasn't helping him. "We ran the plates and the damn thing belongs to Little Donny. How the hell did it get here?"

"Beats me," I said. "Maybe Little Donny drove it over, seeing how it's his car."

Another deputy, one of Blaze's favorites, spotted us from his position by the car, hitched his pants up a notch or two exactly the same way my son did, and strutted over like a rooster.

I groaned.

Deputy Dick Snell, aka Deputy Dickey,

was skinny like a stick and had a face like a coyote, narrow and wily. Animal hair was stuck all over a green blazer that partially covered his wrinkled uniform shirt. At least I guessed it was animal hair, since he didn't have any to spare on his head. The little he did have was greasy and wouldn't have stuck to anything unless he duct taped it there.

He came to a halt next to me and I immediately started sneezing. Cat hair! I'm deathly allergic to cat dander. I backed up a step.

"Don't you worry, ma'am," Deputy Dickey said. "We're in the process of ascertaining who the perpetrator is. Before long he'll be incarcerated and you can sleep easy again."

I hate it when the local boys go away to college. They get big britches — and a vocabulary to match.

"Who are you ascertaining as the killer right this minute?" I looked at Deputy Dickey and his glance fell to the ground.

I sneezed and backed up more.

Blaze butted in. "Ma, let's talk about it later. Go on home."

I watched deputies work over Little Donny's car and I felt a twinge of guilt over not 'fessing up, but for all I knew Blaze might be gathering new evidence about my competence for another go-around in court. I couldn't give him ammunition. Imagine him trying to have me declared incompetent. My own son!

I glanced at Blaze's new sheriff's truck. Someone sat in the front passenger seat.

"I need a ride home," I said to Blaze. "You go finish up. I'll wait for you."

Distracted, Blaze nodded and went into a huddle with Deputy Dickey and Warden Burnett.

I sneezed again. When Blaze didn't notice, I wandered off.

Carl Anderson crouched in the front seat of Blaze's truck. When I opened the door, I could smell the rank chicken grease.

"Spill it, Carl," I said, standing back from the door to escape the fumes.

"Man, oh, man, Gertie. It was awful."

Carl needed a stiff snort of whiskey to calm his tremors.

"I never seen so much blood. And that dead fella laying there missing most of his head."

"Start at the beginning and tell me everything."

"We was sitting out at the bait pile. Little Donny was chowin' down on doughnuts and pretty soon so was I. My stomach started up and before you know it, I had a bellyache you wouldn't believe. So I took the car and went back to the house for my Tums. I usually carry them, what with my bad stomach, but I forgot this morning. Wouldn't ya know, just when I need 'em. And you know how I git. Starts with gas rumbling through my intestines and . . ."

"Okay, okay," I interrupted. The last thing I needed was a graphic description of Carl's bodily functions. "Then what?"

"Then I drove back and found that guy. What was left of him. It was awful."

I thought about giving Carl a pat on the hand or an arm squeeze to let him know everything was going to be okay. But in the warmth of the afternoon the chicken grease fumes radiating from his body were about to knock me flat out.

"What was Little Donny doing through all this?"

"When I left, he was leaning against a tree, cradling his rifle in his arm and stuffing a doughnut in his mouth."

That's my grandson.

"And when I come back," Carl continued, "his rifle was throwed down next to that dead guy, and Little Donny was gone. I called around for him, but he didn't answer. Then I went and got Blaze. But I waited

45

here. I couldn't bring myself to go back in them woods." Carl looked out at the rows of cop cars. "Looks like the whole state of Michigan's police force is here."

I followed Carl's gaze. Deputy Sheedlo, another of Blaze's key deputies, a lardy man with no apparent neck, opened the back of a truck bed and hauled an animal out of a crate. The two of them trotted by, heading for Little Donny's Ford Escort. The animal swung its head in my direction and our eyes met. It was an enormous, black German shepherd with red devil eyes and fangs the size of meat hooks. My blood quit pumping through my overworked, old veins.

I wasn't going to find Little Donny waiting for me at my house, griping at me because I took his wheels. I wouldn't find him at the refrigerator eating me into the poor house.

"Omigod," I whispered to myself, staring at the beast. "They're searching for Little Donny."

THREE

Deputies and volunteers scattered when they saw Devil Fang approaching with Deputy Sheedlo in tow — all except greasy-headed Dickey, who stood waiting with his skinny legs spread wide and his fists clutching the lapels of his hairy green jacket.

Deputy Sheedlo had his hands full, working a few muscles that he didn't normally use just trying to keep the enormous canine from ripping the leash right out of his hands. You could see blue veins bulging on the man's forehead and sweat beads gleaming along his receding hairline.

Deputy Dickey opened the driver's door of Little Donny's Ford Escort and Devil Fang bounded into the car. He did the old sniff-snort around the seat and steering wheel, then No-Neck Sheedlo led him to the edge of the woods and looked back at Dickey.

Devil Fang was sniff-snorting the ground

when Dickey nodded the go-ahead. Sheedlo released the animal from the leash. I was still leaning against the side of Blaze's sheriff's truck watching the action when the light bulb went on in my brain. Since I was the one driving Little Donny's car, my scent was undoubtedly all over it.

Quickly I scooted around the end of Blaze's new truck, heading for the driver's door, when I heard the blood-curdling howl. The hairs on my arms stood up.

I almost made it.

I ripped the door open and reached for the steering wheel with one hand. I even had one foot firmly planted inside before the dog had me by the back of my suspenders. He clamped on and shook his head back and forth, snarling.

Deputy Dickey found us that way. I hung on to the steering wheel for dear life while Devil Fang tried to rip me out by my orange suspenders.

"Get this big, stupid, sorry excuse for a domestic animal off of me," I hollered. "He ripped my new suspender pants."

At a command from Dickey, the animal abruptly let go. I flew face first into the seat of Blaze's truck, catching a blast of Carl's pungent chicken-clothes.

I thought about digging my stun gun out

of my purse and zapping Devil Fang till he was knocked silly, then starting in on Dickey Snell, but I didn't want them to take my stun gun away. It was my chief line of defense until I could get a Glock pistol like a real detective.

I straightened up and adjusted my pants, noting the tear in the suspender. At least I wasn't missing chunks of cloth. Or skin. "Who's in charge of this vicious animal?" I demanded.

No-Neck Sheedlo dragged him away, but it was clear that Devil Fang wasn't giving up easily. He fought the leash and ground his fangs, all the time glaring at me with those beady red eyes. He struggled against the leash until Deputy Dickey stepped in and helped haul him off.

"What is going on here?" I asked Blaze who rushed up and had me by the elbow.

"You okay, Ma?"

"No, I'm not okay. Do I look okay? A rabid police dog has just attacked me for no apparent reason."

"Sit down in the seat and take it easy for a minute."

He helped me up into the truck seat next to Carl. I leaned my head back against the headrest.

"Boy, Gertie," Carl said. "That was something to see." Waves of putrid grease slapped against the air.

"I'm waiting to hear it," I said to Blaze. "Why is every deputy in the U.P. here and what's with the dog? Since when does the sheriff's department use dogs to hunt people?"

Blaze sighed. "The main suspect right now is Little Donny. I know he must have a reasonable explanation for everything, but he left the scene of a crime, his rifle was the murder weapon — at least it looks that way, and his footprints are running every which way through the pools of blood."

"How do you know they're his foot-prints?" I wanted to know.

"Size fourteens."

"Oh." Not many men have size fourteen feet.

But the smoking gun left at the scene of the crime sounded fishy.

"A set-up," I offered. "Little Donny couldn't kill a horsefly even if he set out to do it, and you know it. Somebody's setting him up."

"Then Little Donny needs to come in and tell us what happened. I'm his uncle. Why wouldn't he come to me if he needed help?"

"What if Little Donny's dead?" Carl said.

Blaze glared at him. "Well, Carl, that's

quite an idea you have there. But wouldn't his body be right out in the open for us to find?"

"He's probably at my house watching television right this minute," I suggested.

"He's missing, Ma."

"He's nineteen years old, a teenager." It wasn't too long ago I was changing his diaper and wiping burp-up off my blouse. "What if he's hurt in the woods?"

"We tracked him quite a ways into the woods before we lost trace of him. He wasn't bleeding, or at least he wasn't bleeding hard enough to leave a trail."

I didn't say anything. We had to find Little Donny. It was the first thing Blaze and I had agreed on in a long time.

"Until he shows up, he's the most wanted man in the Upper Peninsula," Blaze finished.

The image of Little Donny's chubby, grinning mug plastered on the walls of every post office in the country flashed through my mind. My eyes filled with tears and I looked away before Blaze noticed.

Little Donny's mother, Heather, was going to have a heart attack if we didn't clear this up right away. The boy needed me. His future, maybe his life, depended on locating him fast.

I had to find Little Donny.

In all the excitement, I forgot that supper was at my house and Grandma Johnson was cooking. I remembered while Blaze was driving me home after dropping Carl at his little shack of a house.

I groaned.

Grandma Johnson is famous for her cooking, and I don't mean in a popular way. Most of us eat before we sit down at one of her meals.

Grandma Johnson is ninety-two and her tongue is poisonous, like a rattlesnake. She's also my mother-in-law. I've never forgiven Barney for dying and leaving me to deal with her. The two of us get along like milk and orange juice. Mix us together and we curdle for sure.

"I have to go home and get Mary and her potato-and-cheese casserole," Blaze said, dropping me at my front door. "I'll bring her, but she'll need a ride home from somebody later."

"Aren't you coming, too?"

"Not with a murder in our backyard and my nephew missing."

I didn't feel too much like eating, either. My body felt as if every organ was tied in double knots.

After Blaze drove off, I stood on my porch and assessed the damage that my tromping around in the woods all day had done to my grooming. I swatted some of the dog hair off my pants and patted my own hair once or twice. I wasn't sure why I was bothering, since Grandma Johnson was about to work me over, no matter what.

I opened the screen door and walked into the living room. The door snapped shut behind me with a bang like my twelve-gauge shotgun going off, but Grandma didn't hear it. She was watching the local news on television and had the volume cranked up as high as it would go.

Little Donny's high-school class picture, smeared across the television set bold as brass, reminded me that he hadn't changed much in the last year. The announcer finished up as Grandma spotted me at the door.

"Can't nobody come by and warn me when something like this happens?" Grandma crabbed. "Breaking news bulletin, they say, and so I run in here from the kitchen, and what do I see? A dead man being hauled out of the woods and my great-grandson wanted for questioning. You . . ." Grandma shook a crooked finger in my direction. "You will be the death of me just

53

like you were the death of my boy."

Grandma's comments are outrageous, figments of a warped imagination. I've learned to ignore them.

All the while she was complaining, she gave me the evil eye. I helped her get up from the sofa after watching her rock back and forth trying to get momentum on her own. She gripped my offered hand with her own, cold and bony like the remains of a scaled fish.

"It's all a misunderstanding," I shouted over the television noise. "I'm helping with the case and so I'm in on some information that the general public doesn't have. Trust me, Little Donny's not in any trouble. Ask Blaze, if you don't believe me."

"I would if I could find him. At least he'd tell me the truth."

Grandma Johnson is shriveled up like an old apple you'd find in the back of your refrigerator when you finally decide to clean it out. One that's so old and moldy it takes a few seconds to identify it. And she smells like a nursing home, which is where I keep suggesting we put her. No one else agrees with me. Yet. That's because they aren't the ones having to deal with her all the time.

I don't know why Grandma showed up on my doorstep with her suitcase. Unless she planned to drive me crazy.

The only thing that looks new on Grandma Johnson is her dentures, which really are brand-spanking new. She wore an old faded housedress with an apron tied around her waist and she snapped her new teeth.

"I better go check my bird," she said, "before I go burning it up. Almost forgot it in all the excitement."

She sent one last glare my way and headed for the kitchen. I shut off the television, then followed her and watched as she opened the oven door. Holding hot pads in both hands, she carefully pulled the roasting pan out of the oven. My mother-in-law set it on top of the stove and removed the cover.

"See there," she said. "I did almost burn it."

I looked over her shoulder and couldn't help noticing the chicken was so rare it could almost fly away. I also noticed that she had forgotten to turn on the oven. I made a mental note to buy a microwave for times like this.

Maybe after the family digs into this chicken, they'll agree with me about the nursing home.

The supper table was quiet for a change.

Star, my youngest at forty-one, sat next to me looking as pretty as a bouquet of pink four-o'-clocks. Even her lipstick and toenail polish were pink to match her outfit. I look out for her the best I can since I still think of her as my baby, so I was sharing the plastic bag I held on my lap. She and I were tossing raw chicken into it and watching the others work on figuring out what to do with theirs.

"Take a big bite of Grandma's chicken," I said to Mary, the chief opponent to placing Grandma in a nursing home but the last to offer to take her in. "It's real good."

Grandma was crabbing as usual and forgetting to eat.

"It's a disgrace to our family," she said, "and I want it fixed right now. Someone better fix this mess Gertie made."

I wasn't sure why I was getting the blame for Little Donny's problems, but I kept quiet.

I smiled at Mary and Star, who nodded and shook their heads in unison whenever appropriate. I missed Blaze at the table. His cheeks would be filled with potato-and-cheese casserole. Between bites he'd be pontificating, mostly rubbish and self-important blab, but occasionally he'd drop bits of information I could use.

"I don't know why we're sitting here, stuffing our faces. Shouldn't we be out looking for Little Donny?" I said to no one in particular.

"He'll turn up. Soon as he gets hungry," Star said.

"He's probably lost in the woods by now," I said, pushing away my full plate.

Grandma Johnson clicked her new teeth at me. "Barney must be turning over in his grave, what with you carrying on, causing trouble everywhere you go. Are you still associatin' with that man-hungry woman?"

"Cora Mae isn't man-hungry. She's just spunky."

"In my day a woman like that would'a been drove out of town loaded down with hot tar and turkey feathers."

"Have a bite of chicken," I said to her. "It's real good, the best you ever made."

Everyone had gone home and Grandma Johnson was in bed when I walked outside and turned my face to the starry sky. A flash of metal drew my attention earthward. A sheriff's truck was attempting to hide on the side of my driveway under a tall pine tree. Deputy Sheedlo peered out at me from the driver's seat when I approached.

"You go ahead and take a nice nap," I said

to him. "If Little Donny shows up, I'll wake you."

"My shift's over in a bit. I'll make it."

Back inside, I almost expected to find my grandson snoring away in the spare bedroom. I fought the urge to call his name through the house. His room didn't appear to have been touched since morning.

Wondering how to tell my other daughter the bad news about her son, I decided to wait one more day in case things straightened out. Chances were, Heather wasn't getting Michigan news way down in Milwaukee. She might as well have one last good night's sleep before I had to tell her that her son was missing and a man had been murdered.

I didn't have a clue where to start looking for Little Donny. When I couldn't stand the quiet any longer I picked up the phone.

"Cora Mae, we have work to do tomorrow," I said. "You need to come by with my new truck. We'll take it over to George's for some rewiring."

I knew that mentioning George would work. Cora Mae would love to get her man-hungry — I mean spunky — hooks into that hunk of a man.

"What about George?" she asked, coyly. "You two going out?"

58

Once, George and I went to a movie in Escanaba, and it felt awkward and uncomfortable. We were best friends, but all of a sudden we didn't know what to say to each other.

"It's way too early for me to think about dating, Cora Mae."

"It's been over two years. Time to move on."

"I don't want to ruin my friendship with George. If we go out and it doesn't work out, things will never be the same."

There was a pause on the other end of the line, then Cora Mae said in a sweet, confidential voice, "Mind if I give him a try?"

"Go ahead," I said, but I didn't mean it. I wasn't a sexy woman like Cora Mae. What could George see in little old me that he couldn't find more of in my friend? Unless he appreciated brains over beauty.

Because I didn't want to be alone with my thoughts I kept Cora Mae on the phone as long as I could, going on about small things that didn't really matter in the face of Little Donny's disappearance.

Eventually, Cora Mae hung up, and I spent the night listening for the sound of a door opening.

It never did.

FOUR

Tuesday morning, after a sleepless night, I found Little Donny's mother, Heather, and her husband, Big Donny, pounding on my door. It was long before the sun was up. The moon was still visible over the horizon, and the guinea hens were still roosting in the trees. Usually they hear when someone pulls into the driveway, and they come running, squawking up a storm. You have to be up early to beat those hens, and Heather was.

My daughter blew into the room like a tornado and threw herself at me, sobbing and wailing. Big Donny blustered after her, bogged down with enough suitcases to last the winter.

I unwrapped Heather's death grip from my neck and deposited her on a kitchen chair with a box of tissues while I made coffee and popped frozen cinnamon rolls into the oven.

"Milwaukee's five hours away," I said. "You must have started out before midnight."

"Blaze called and told us about Little Donny." Heather's sobs were turning into hiccups. "I couldn't sleep from the worry so we packed up and started driving. Is there any news?"

"Not yet."

Big Donny dove into the cinnamon rolls with the same determination as his son would have. After he'd swallowed three without chewing, I put two on a plate for Heather for when she felt like eating again, and took one for myself. I handed mine to Big Donny after I noticed him eyeing his empty plate.

"I'll pop a few more in the oven," I said. "It'll only take a few minutes."

Big Donny wasn't big, just like Little Donny wasn't little. Big Donny stood about five-foot-five in his brown wingtips, but he made up for it in girth. He's almost as wide as he is tall, with a short-guy complex the size of his white Lincoln Continental. A carnivore, he absolutely loves meat and potatoes, as long as they don't touch each other on the plate. He looks down his nose at those who hunt and tend gardens for their survival.

He's a stockbroker in downtown Milwaukee, and his meat has to come from the grocery store, preferably from one of those specialty stores, and his oversized suits have to be Italian.

Little Donny, on the other hand, appreciates his Swedish, backwoods heritage, and when I get done with him, he'll be shooting the knobs off clothespins on the clothesline. Even though I don't hunt, I know how to hold a rifle, and I can shoot straight if I put my mind to it.

"You don't look the worse for wear," I observed, watching Big Donny pound down my share of cinnamon rolls.

"Heather was so worked up I had her drive. I slept most of the way. No use both of us suffering from lack of sleep."

Big Donny always has been an insensitive oaf.

Heather looked a mess. Her eyes were just about puffed shut and her hair looked like a rat's nest. I helped her get comfortable while Donny dragged in more suitcases from his fancy Lincoln.

The guinea hens eventually discovered the Lincoln intruder and shouted and flapped around the car. I threw some feed behind the shed and told them to scat, but they ignored me.

The guinea hens and I have learned to get along, but it took awhile. At first I thought they were like chickens, but guineas are much more independent, which is why I like them so much. They don't take well to confinement and neither do I. We have an understanding. They'll hang around and eat bugs, especially wood ticks, which I hate, as long as I don't try to coop them up inside chicken wire.

Guinea hens take their chances in the treetops through the night, and occasionally a conniving raccoon will outsmart one of them, but it's rare. During the day, when they aren't snacking on bugs, they stand guard in the front yard against automobiles attempting to encroach on their territory.

I was out in the driveway having my "bug off" conversation with the hens when Blaze's sheriff truck pulled in, followed by another truck full of deputies. A slew of uniforms piled out and I noticed Devil Fang's cage in the truck bed.

The guineas must have spotted the dog too, because they cleared out.

I groaned as Deputy Sheedlo hauled the animal out under Dickey Snell's supervision.

"What are you planning on doing with

that pathetic excuse for a search dog?" I asked.

Deputy Dickey puffed up his skinny rooster chest. "This superb police dog will locate the suspect once he acquires the proper scent. He's trained for this line of investigation."

"The suspect?" I shouted at Dickey. "By suspect do you mean my grandson? I'll suspect you, you little twerp."

Blaze grabbed my elbow and pulled me back.

"We're still trying to get a good scent going." Blaze hitched up his pants over his potbelly with his free hand. The weight of the gun on his hip was helping to send them south.

I looked at my son's gun. "Little Donny's still missing." It wasn't a question.

Blaze nodded.

"He hasn't called here. I was hoping he'd at least call and let us know he's okay."

"No one's heard a thing, Ma."

"Your sister and her husband are inside, and I don't want them more upset than they already are. Take that vicious animal and get out of here." I pointed at Deputy Sheedlo. "Go on, put that thing away."

"No can do," Blaze said, demonstrating his remarkable grasp of the English language. "The dog needs to help find Little Donny. What if he's hurt in the woods and can't find his way out? The dog can help, Ma."

I hadn't thought of that, and I didn't want to think of it now. With mixed feelings, I let them inside, and Blaze led the way to the spare bedroom where Little Donny slept. Big Donny and Heather watched from the hall, and when Heather realized what was going on, the dam broke again. I would have to put tissues on my grocery list.

"What's goin' on out here?" Grandma Johnson shuffled out of her room, forgetting her new teeth in the excitement. Devil Fang and several weighty deputies almost ran her over. Blaze threw out an arm to protect Grandma. "In there," he said, nodding toward the spare room.

Devil Fang went right to the jacket that I'd rummaged through to find Little Donny's keys. Another battle started between the dog and me. Blaze jumped in between us and I managed to kick him in the shin. The dog, excited now and not sure whose side he should be on, grabbed Blaze's other pant leg. Blaze howled. Heather screamed.

The ruckus ended as quickly as it had started.

The cops stared at Devil Fang, clearly

puzzled by the dumb dog's inability to tell the difference between Little Donny and a crusty old woman.

"He's getting up there in years," Dickey explained, defensively. "I was thinking about retiring him next year, but at this rate, he'll be grazing sooner than planned."

I grinned at Devil Fang. That'll teach the mangy mutt.

Blaze reached over and patted Devil Fang's head. "Good boy, Fred."

"Fred? That's his name?" I couldn't believe this aggressive mass of hooked fangs could be called that.

I pulled the bedsheet from the bed, balled it up, and gave it to Blaze. "This'll give Fred a good start. Now get going. You're riling Heather."

Cora Mae was hanging all over George something terrible.

"I just love tools," she said, eyeing his groin and standing so close to him they looked like Siamese twins.

She'd been after him without snagging him for the longest time. Cora Mae usually gets what she wants right away. George is her first holdout and, true to form, she wasn't handling it well and was acting more aggressive than usual, especially after my reluctant permission.

George slid back his cowboy hat with the coiled rattlesnake on the brim. He wore a tight white undershirt and snug blue jeans, and I figured, if you're going to dress like that around Cora Mae, you're just asking for trouble.

To tell the truth, I've never seen a sixty-year-old man look so good. George Erikson and I have had a special friendship, relaxed and easy, ever since his wife picked up and left him on Christmas Eve the year before last, and I didn't want Cora Mae busting in and ruining it.

George was my best friend after Cora Mae, and I wanted to keep it that way. I felt a twinge of irritation every time I thought of them maybe getting together.

George slapped a wrench into Cora Mae's hand. "I sprayed oil on those rusty bolts," he said, pointing at my new truck's strobe lights. "Give it a minute to work, then see if you can pry them loose."

By the look on Cora Mae's face, the wrench in her hand wasn't the tool she loved so much.

George winked at me.

I hid a grin and went to work opening the lettering kit and arranging the letters on the ground.

Cora Mae and I had had a heated discussion on the way over to George's house about the name of our company. I won, since starting the business was my idea, and to top it off, it was *my* truck. She wanted to go over every little contribution she had made. I acknowledged her points, but still won because it was *my* truck.

Putting lettering on the side of a truck is harder than it looks. I stood back and viewed my work. THE TROUBLE BUSTERS. The letters swayed and swerved along the passenger side of the truck. I tried to peel a few off and set them right, but they were already cemented on like dried concrete.

I did a little better on the driver's side. By the time I finished, George had the lights and siren in working order, and we were ready for business.

I gave him a quick cheek kiss and pulled Cora Mae toward the truck before she could give him her version of the same.

We bounced along a gravel road north of town with the lights and siren going just for fun. "Where are we going?" Cora Mae asked.

I shouted back over the blare of the siren, "We're going to have to interrogate the bear hunters camped in the area where the murder occurred. Maybe someone saw something."

I turned onto the rutted dirt road leading to Walter Laakso's house, remembering at the last minute to warn Cora Mae about his typically friendly greetings to visitors.

Walter barreled out the front door with his sawed-off shotgun leveled directly at me. Cora Mae had decided to wait in the truck till introductions were over.

"Dang," I said, stepping away from the truck, my hands in the air. "It's Gertie Johnson. Put that thing away. Do we have to go through this every time I come to visit?"

"Hey, Gertie," Walter said, glancing at the passenger window and frowning. The shotgun didn't waver, it just redirected. "Who's that with ya?"

"That's Cora Mae. Come on out, Cora Mae. It's safe."

After Walter lowered the gun, she slid out of the seat and followed us inside. We sat at the kitchen table while Walter boiled a fresh pot of coffee on the stove. He poured coffee all around, then dumped brandy in his and added some to Cora Mae's before she knew what was happening. I spread my hand over the rim of my cup to ward him off.

"No thanks," I said. "I'm on the job."

Walter gave me a wide grin, exposing the gaps where his front teeth used to be.

I looked around. Walter's place was what you'd expect from an old guy who's lived in the backwoods alone pretty much all his life. Piles of dirty dishes lined the counter and the kitchen table was littered with tools, cans of bug spray, and other health hazards.

Walter scratched his long scrawny beard, took a sip of his coffee-laced brandy, and asked about my husband.

"Barney's been dead a few years now, Walter. You remember, don't you? You came to the funeral."

"Oh, ya," he said. Then waited.

Small talk is an art in the Michigan U.P., since most things that happen here are small. Long silences are okay, too. Most of what's said will be said again tomorrow. The weather, gardening, and the no-good federal government are all good topics, interspersed with pauses and throat clearings. It's our way of life.

Only I wasn't here for small talk.

"A warden was killed yesterday. You hear anything about that?"

"Just that he's dead," Walter said.

"Who told you?" I sipped my coffee, noticing Cora Mae hadn't touched hers. She'd slid her chair back as far from the table as

70

possible.

"The Detroit boys came in from the bait pile early yesterday. They knew."

"You're still renting out bait piles to out-of-towners?"

Walter nodded.

"Where are they staying?"

"I've got a trailer out back."

Leasing chunks of land to hunters is common practice around Stonely. There aren't many jobs to speak of, and taxes have to be paid on the properties, so some people have resorted to renting to the city boys, most of them coming from Chicago or Detroit. However, it's not a popular way to add income, and those who do it generally don't make announcements to the community.

"My grandson seems to be missing," I continued. "Anybody around here see him?"

Walter shook his head back and forth. He rolled up the sleeves of his worn, red flannel shirt and took a long gulp of his coffee. I noticed red welts skittering over his arms.

"Looks like you got yourself into a mess of stinging nettles," I said.

"I was sicklin' brush over on the side of the south fence, and must'a got in it there. Didn't even notice till I was done. Stuff runs for miles all along the fencing on that side."

Stinging nettle can grow as tall as a large

man. It looks wispy and harmless along the edges of clearings, snuggling up against fences and outbuildings where people tend to walk. Then it waits patiently for some poor sucker to come wading through it. If you rub up against it, small hairs poke through your exposed skin injecting formic acid, the welts leap up, and the itching starts and goes on forever.

I heard you can boil and eat the new growth of a stinging nettle — that could come in handy if you were lost and starving. Boiling supposedly neutralizes the acid. Of course, you'd need a pair of gloves to pick it and a pot to boil it in, which aren't convenient items to locate out in the woods.

Lost and starving reminded me of my mission.

"I need to find Little Donny," I said, draining my coffee. "Maybe the Detroit boys know something useful. How many piles are they sitting on?"

Walter scratched his welts. "Three. But they're buried deep. Can't drive your truck in."

"No, but your ATV ought to do just dandy."

The ATV was painted in camouflage, or camo as we like to call it. Brown with large green leaves. And it roared like a souped-up race car down the path Walter had pointed out to us.

"Hang on tight," I called over my shoulder to Cora Mae as I opened up the machine on a straight stretch. "Let's see what it'll do."

I was having so much fun, I almost blew right past the first bait pile.

Pre-work is everything in bear hunting. Since a bear travels in a circuit ranging from several days to several weeks, a hunter tries to hold him in an area as long as possible by enticing him with tantalizing treats. The smellier, the better.

I smelled the pile before I saw it.

Pulling over, I crawled off the ATV, adjusted my oversized weapons handbag on my shoulder, and began surveying the site.

The Detroit boys sat like ants on a log and watched. Cora Mae noticed them immediately. She patted her hair and re-tucked her blouse. Then she made more detailed clothing adjustments, slowing down for their benefit, opening a button on her blouse, and fanning herself like she was overheating.

"Oh, for God's sake," I snorted. "Give it a rest."

They must have heard us coming a long

way off, which is the disadvantage of the ATV mode of travel. You aren't going to be sneaking up on anybody. I suppose I looked pretty ridiculous driving up in blazing orange and freshly mended suspender pants riding on a camo ATV, but they didn't notice my attire since they were all staring at Cora Mae, the sandwiches clutched in their paws forgotten.

I have to give it to Cora Mae. She can turn a man's head no matter his age. He can be twenty years older or twenty years younger than she is. She's definitely got sex appeal.

These three men were in their early fifties, give or take a few years, and they looked alike. Large round faces and large facial features with big honking noses and wide-set eyes.

"Hey, boys," Cora Mae called, strolling over, apparently in her element. "Let's introduce ourselves."

The boys turned out to be brothers — Marlin Smith, Remy Smith, and BB Smith — and none too bright. Detroit schools must not turn out too many rocket scientists. But I had to admire the creativity of their parents. While I'd named Blaze, Heather, and Star after horses, the Detroit boys were named after firearms.

"It smells like someone died," I said, after

making sure the odor wasn't floating over from the boys. "What a stench."

They seemed to notice me for the first time. Marlin pointed at a five-gallon bucket hanging from a large tree branch. "Walter goes smelting in the spring, throws a bunch of them in a bucket, seals it, and lets it sit all summer in the garage. Then we string it up and I shoot a hole in it with my twenty-two so it dribbles out onto the ground. Have to shoot a hole a little lower every day to keep it dripping. Works like a charm."

I scrunched my nose. "See any action yet?"

"Not yet, but somebody has. Been hearing shots on and off all morning."

BB grinned at Cora Mae. "How about some lunch?"

Cora Mae and I settled in with turkey sandwiches and cold Budweiser beers. We traded dumb bear stories for a while before I got to the point.

"A warden was killed out this way yesterday," I said.

"Good riddance to bad rubbish," Marlin said with a nasty little smirk. His brothers laughed.

"You know the guy?"

Remy chimed in, through a mouth packed with bread. "Don't need to, they're all alike.

DNR agents used to be hunters, meaning once upon a time they thought like hunters, like us. Now they're all a bunch of tree huggers with fancy degrees."

I nodded. "Yup. The DNR's been infiltrated by those Sierra guys."

"And don't ask the DNR anything, or right away they want to arrest you," BB Smith added.

I glanced at him sharply. "Someone want to arrest you?"

BB looked startled. "Uh, no."

"My grandson's lost out here," I said, taking a bite of my turkey sandwich and noticing Marlin frown at BB. "You guys see a kid about nineteen?"

"Some guy walked through here coupla hours ago," Marlin said. "Just said howdy and moved on through, heading that way." Marlin pointed down the path in the opposite direction from Walter's place.

I was excited. "Was he big and wearing orange?"

"Yep," Marlin said, taking a swig of beer. "That was him all right."

I jumped up and pried Cora Mae away from an eyeball stare she had going with BB Smith. "Come on, Cora Mae, I know that was him."

"Half the men around here are wearing

76

orange. It could be anybody." Cora Mae brushed herself off, slowly running her hands over the front of her blouse. BB actually drooled.

"Gotta go," I said, heading for the ATV with Cora Mae in tow. I thought of something and turned back. "Has the sheriff been through asking questions?"

"You're the first."

Figures. I'm always one step ahead of my son. He must be too busy doggy sitting to do any real investigating.

"I don't know what it is about you, Cora Mae," I said as we thundered down a wide trail used by snowmobiles in the winter. "You always manage to pick out the dumbest one in the pack, quite a feat considering the limited choices back there."

"Nothing at all wrong with dumb," Cora Mae replied.

The other two bait piles were pretty much like the first. The Smith brothers had strung smelt buckets at each of them, so it wasn't any trouble finding them. We followed our noses. The piles were deserted for the moment, since all the boys were together and busy stuffing their faces. There was no sign of Little Donny.

Cora Mae held a white embroidered

hanky over her nose and mouth and mumbled. "Big and wearing orange isn't much to go on."

"It was him," I insisted. "I have a feeling."

We drove past the last of Walter's piles and came to a fork in the trail. Normally we'd have to make a decision about which way was the correct one, but in our case, it was handled for us. The ATV conked out right at the fork, and refused to start up again.

I jumped off and checked the gas. Bone dry.

"You'd think," I said to Cora Mae, "Walter could have made sure we had enough gas."

Cora Mae didn't speak, just looked up at the treetops and frowned. I followed her gaze and saw rain clouds forming above us in dark, angry swirls. The birds were flittering past, heading for cover.

"You didn't happen to bring an umbrella?" I said, perching my Blublocker sunglasses on the top of my head.

Apparently Cora Mae was giving me the silent treatment, like it was my fault we were out of gas and stranded in a thunderstorm.

The sky opened up and pelted us with large, wet drops.

"Head for the trees," I called, and we scampered for the canopy. I tried holding my handbag over my head for protection, but almost conked myself silly from the weight of the weapons landing on my head. Almost broke my sunglasses, too.

Cora Mae had on those strapped sandals with high heels she's so fond of, so I reached the trees ahead of her.

That's why I was first to spot the body.

I crammed four white knuckles into my mouth to stop the scream rising in my throat. My knees buckled beneath me and I leaned heavily against a tree for support. I slid down the tree and sat there with my legs straight out in front of me.

Life passed before my eyes just like they say it does when you're near the end. Only it wasn't my life snuffed out.

Was it Little Donny?

I thought of my favorite grandson visiting every summer since he was a little tyke, wanting to know everything there was to know about hunting and fishing. Always was the curious one, wanting to go back to the beginning, to his roots. He wasn't one for that fancy Milwaukee city life Heather forced on him. I'd been hoping that one day soon he'd move to Stonely and live close by.

I saw movement out of the corner of my eye and Cora Mae came into focus. She

79

brushed past me and walked toward the body, which was lying face down partially covered by a pile of leaves.

Two long arrows jutted out of the dead man's back.

Cora Mae floated in slow motion, blocking my view, then she was hauling on his jacket from the back and moving around to his other side and pushing, struggling to turn him enough so she could see his face. She pushed and shoved for a long time. To give her credit, she could be tough as toenails when she had to be.

The whole time, all I could do was watch in helpless terror.

Eventually, I saw him flop back down, the arrows solidly planted. Cora Mae stood up and said something to me, but it sounded garbled, like listening to the radio between two stations. My ears felt plugged up and I had to grip my lower lip with my top teeth to stop the shaking.

I blinked fast several times and that seemed to help. "What?" I squeaked.

"It's Billy Lundberg," Cora Mae called.

"Billy Lundberg, the drunk?"

"How many Billy Lundbergs you think live around here?" Cora Mae had her hands on her hips, dark mascara streaks washing down her cheeks with the rain.

My knees were still weak when I pushed off from the tree and stumbled over to get a good look to make sure. Looking down, I felt a little guilty over the relief I was experiencing that Billy was dead, not Little Donny. And I was feeling giddy over being the first investigator at a crime scene.

Billy had been the town drunk since way back. He lived alone after his wife got disgusted with his bad habits, packed up the kids, and disappeared. Billy might have been socially dysfunctional, but he was a regular churchgoer. A Catholic, if I remembered right.

Billy had seen his last confessional.

"He's not stiff yet," I noted. "Must have happened this morning."

His head was turned to the side. I tried to close his eyes for him like I'd seen on television, but they wouldn't go.

"The eyes are the first things to stiffen up," I explained to Cora Mae, wondering if I was right.

We were standing side by side over Billy, both shocked and thinking about what to do next. The rain wasn't letting up, but it didn't matter anymore. The two of us looked like we'd just climbed out of Lake Michigan after a nice swim with our clothes on. Cora Mae's top was plastered to her chest and her jet-black hair was hanging around her face in little dripping curls.

A steady mixture of blood and rain slithered away from the body.

"Give me a hand," I said, wiping water from my face. "We better search him."

"Touching a dead body gives me the willies."

"You just about bear-mauled him a few minutes ago." Cora Mae's been around more dead bodies than anyone I know. She buried three husbands and every one of them she found dead by herself.

"All right," Cora Mae agreed. "I'll check his pants."

Figures.

Billy wasn't carrying much — a ring of keys, a wallet with two dollars and a driver's license, and a pocketknife. A travel mug tipped on its side lay next to the body. I didn't have to sniff too close to the rim to know it had been filled with straight whiskey.

"Wonder what Billy was doing way out here?" Cora Mae said.

"Probably got too drunk to find his way out. He's done it before." I studied the two arrows jutting from his back and walked around to try to follow traces of blood. "Looks like he crawled for a while."

I watched the rain begin to wash away the trail.

"Let's get out of here," Cora Mae said.

We started down the path leading out of the woods. I guessed it was going to be quite a hike. But we hadn't gone twenty yards when I heard thrashing in among the trees, a few loud shouts, and a bone-chilling howl.

Blaze and No-Neck Sheedlo came stumbling out of the brush, pulled rapidly by frothing Fred. Fred was straining against the lead in the direction of Billy Lundberg's body, and the two fat boys were struggling to slow the beast down.

Blaze was too winded to say a word, which is just how I like him. He leaned over and gasped.

"Any luck?" I asked. "Finding anything unusual out in the woods, son? You ought to have the case almost solved, what with that smart dog and all."

I waited patiently for Blaze to catch his breath. Sheedlo wrapped the end of the leash around a small tree and knotted it. Fred, temporarily forgetting his mission, got busy peeing on each side of the tree. When he finished marking the tree, he apparently remembered why he was out here in the first place and started lunging against the leash.

"Haven't found Little Donny yet, if that's

what you're asking," Blaze managed to wheeze. His wet pants clung to his chunky legs, which were splattered with mud clear up to his knees. "What in the world are you two doing out here, Ma?"

"Visiting."

"Fred picked up Little Donny's scent and we followed it for a while," Blaze said, raggedly, pointing vaguely into the woods. "Then he lost it. We were just about ready to quit and call it a day when Fred let loose, howling and carrying on."

Blaze sat down on a fallen tree, and I noticed the rain had stopped. I could see the squall moving away as quickly as it had appeared, leaving us soaked and chilled.

Blaze took off his sheriff's hat and wiped his face with his arm.

"This is too much like work for me," he said. "Never been much of a runner." Or a walker, swimmer, or exerciser, I thought. Anything requiring calorie loss scared Blaze.

I heard a rifle shot in the distance. Then another.

Fred began making more racket than an uninvited raccoon in a coop full of chickens.

"We came from down the road," I said, studying the lunging dog. "No sign of Little Donny, but that's the least of your problems right now. I think you'll need that . . ." I pointed at the cell phone attached to Blaze's belt. I paused for effect. "You're gonna want to call for help with poor Billy Lundberg. He's lying in the leaves back that way."

"Dead drunk again, I suppose," Blaze said.

"Something like that," I said.

FIVE

Deputy Dickey arrived with his entourage, wearing the same jacket he'd worn yesterday. His hair looked one day greasier too. Dickey managed to drive down the trail followed by a sheriff's pickup truck. Volunteer deputies hung out of every window and came swarming out of the truck bed when it stopped. A dead man in the woods brings out the entire community.

Cora Mae and I gave statements while the pickup truck tried to back down the trail to find the Detroit boys for questioning. Later, BB and Marlin appeared, each driving an ATV. They wandered over to watch.

Deputy Dickey strutted over to them. "This is a containment field. Important evidence is being gathered. You'll have to move out." He gestured to a volunteer, who stepped closer to let the Smith boys know they meant business. The boys went back to their ATVs and Cora Mae and I followed them.

"Cops are all over our camp," Marlin said to Cora Mae, "like flies on duct tape. You wouldn't believe how many questions they asked us."

Cora Mae put her hand on BB's shoulder. "How about a ride out of here, Big Boy?"

Cora Mae's been watching too many old movies, but BB appreciated it. He smiled wide.

"Hop on."

Cora Mae snuggled behind BB on his ATV and I climbed up behind Marlin, clutching my weapon handbag tightly between us. One false move from the Detroit boy and he'd be rolling on the ground, zapped with my trusty stun gun. "We're going home," I called to Blaze.

"Might as well," Blaze said. "We'll let you know if we need you."

I thought my boy looked tired. Working on a case involving his own nephew was wearing on him. It was starting to wear on me too.

We drove along the trail to Walter's place to pick up my truck, and I found myself worrying about Little Donny's safety. Was he hungry and wet from the rainstorm? He'd disappeared twenty-four hours ago, and the only thing to show for my efforts to help him was another dead body. My muscles knotted in tension around my heart. What if Little Donny turned out to be the killer's next victim?

We pulled into Walter's yard. I was shivering from the wet clothes and windy ride. The temperature had dropped since noon.

Cora Mae eased off the ATV. "What does BB stand for?"

"Bazooka," BB said, puffing up his chest. "A bazooka launches rockets, like in those war movies."

Marlin snorted. "Don't believe him. He was named for those little bitty shot pellets you shoot rabbits with."

"Was not."

"Was too."

I walked away shaking my head. I knew exactly what BB stood for — Bottom of the Brain Barrel.

They were still arguing when I went up to Walter's door. Walter met me with his sawed-off shotgun hanging loose from his arm.

After giving him directions on where to pick up his ATV, we headed out. I was plumb tuckered out, physically and emotionally.

My friend Kitty stood on her front porch

Wednesday morning wearing a tent-sized, yellow housedress that exposed her dimpled knees. Her pin-curled head bobbed as she waved one slab-of-beef arm over her head. At least ten years younger than Cora Mae and me, she was ten years ahead of us in the falling apart department.

Kitty thinks of herself as my part-time bodyguard whenever it suits her. I don't really need a bodyguard and I don't pay her. The bodyguard job is her way of finding a reason to hang around with us. Not only is she the town gossip and knows everything going on, but I discovered she also has worthwhile connections in surrounding towns.

Kitty's yard looks like the town dump. Whenever something wears out she opens the front door and heaves it into the yard. The town's after her to clean it up, but so far nothing has changed.

I stepped over a plastic bucket and followed her inside.

Cora Mae helped herself to a sugar doughnut from a plate on the kitchen table and plopped down.

"How's Heather holding up?" Kitty wanted to know.

"Okay, considering."

"I made a nice carrot cake for you to take

home. You have enough to worry about without having to cook for the whole bunch. Is anyone helping you?"

"Thanks. I appreciate it. Heather will pitch in."

Kitty sat on a kitchen chair and I braced for the collapse I was sure would follow. The chair held, but she spread her chunky legs, exposing more than anyone would care to see. I looked away. "Let's go over what we know," she said. "This certainly is a kerfuffle."

Her eyes slid to me.

Kitty and I have an unspoken but ongoing word battle raging. Ever since she discovered my word-for-the-day routine, she's been throwing big words around. When I realized I wouldn't remember most of the new vocabulary I was trying to learn, I decided to abandon that daily routine even though I love discovering new words. But Kitty won't quit baiting me.

Sometimes it's fun, other times I'd like to pitch her off a Lake Superior cliff.

"I have one important question that has me fomented," I said, zinging one right back at her. "What was a warden from Marquette doing way down here?"

"Maybe they wander all over," Cora Mae suggested.

"You'd think they have their own territories to cover." I blew on my coffee and took a sip. "Like sheriffs or firefighters. I don't think this one just woke up early yesterday and decided to drive south to visit Carl's bait pile."

"Maybe he had a tip," Cora Mae offered.

"So," I said, feeling the sharp heat of uncontrollable tension. "Carl and Little Donny were in cahoots on something illegal. Is that right, Cora Mae?" Cora Mae opened her mouth to say something. I barreled on. "The warden surprises Little Donny, who is caught holding the bag. Little Donny blows the warden's head off and escapes. Then just for fun, he pops a few arrows into the town drunk's back. Is that pretty much it?"

Cora Mae looked at me with wide eyes. I realized my nerves were showing and I was taking my stress out on my best friend, but I couldn't stop.

"Of course I don't think that," she said, sounding hurt. "I'm just trying to help."

She had her hands cupped around her coffee. I reached over and squeezed them to let her know I didn't mean to hurt her feelings. She smiled. It's hard to keep Cora Mae down.

I leaned on the table and rubbed my face with both hands. I voiced my fears. "What if Little Donny's dead?"

Kitty took over. "Don't be ridiculous. He witnessed a murder, is my bet. He probably ate too many sweet rolls and took a snooze in the bushes. The killer didn't even see him. Probably walked up and saw Little Donny's rifle leaning against a tree and used it. The bang woke up Little Donny, he panicked, then ran off. He's good and lost by now, but we'll find him."

I was feeling better. Kitty's theory made sense. It would be like Little Donny to run away and get lost. After all, he's a city boy and they can't tell directions.

"Why didn't he run right to Blaze?" I asked.

"Because he's lost."

"What about Billy?" Cora Mae put in her two cents. "Who would have shot him full of arrows?"

That made no sense to me either. We both looked at Kitty like she had all the answers.

"I don't know," Kitty said. "But we'll find out." She grinned, her teeth gleaming. Kitty's teeth are the whitest in the county.

That reminded me.

I dug the red tooth from my pocket and laid it on the table. "I found this in the brush at Carl's bait pile."

Kitty picked the tooth up, studying it.

92

"What is it?"

"An Indian arrowhead?" Cora Mae guessed.

"Looks like a tooth to me." Kitty handed it to Cora Mae. "But why's it red?"

"Berry stains," Cora Mae said, indifferently. "Bears eat berries, don't they?" She handed the tooth back to me. "No big deal."

"You eat berries, too," I said. "Are your teeth red? And what is a bear tooth doing in the brush? A bear will generally keep his teeth in his mouth from what I hear."

"Don't lose it. We'll put on our thinking caps and come up with something," Cora Mae said.

"Oh. I have a surprise for you." Kitty rubbed her hands together with glee. Her arm blubber bounced. "I've got us a meeting at the morgue in Escanaba tomorrow."

"With the coroner who worked on Robert Hendricks?" I squealed.

"Well not exactly the coroner, but someone who can get us in."

"How'd you do that?" Cora Mae asked.

"I keep trying to tell you. I have men chasing me around all the time. I met him at a social a while back."

I looked at Kitty's enormous body and pin-curled hair, which she rarely combed out, and I wanted to hug her to death.

My main goal was to get Little Donny back in one healthy piece, but discovering the killer might lead the way to Little Donny. We had to cover all the angles and chase every clue.

Blaze pulled into Kitty's yard behind my truck, blocking my plans for a hasty escape. Big Donny sat next to him.

"How's Heather?" I asked Big Donny when he jumped down.

"The doctor prescribed a sedative for her. She's resting. We've been looking all over for you."

I couldn't help noticing Blaze was circling my truck like a turkey vulture homing in on fresh meat. His face was tomato-red. That's what happens when he gets worked up, which is just about always.

"How did you manage to find this piece of junk?" he roared, referring to his old sheriff truck — the one I now legally owned.

"I bought it at the auction in Escanaba and fixed it up a bit. Looks pretty good, doesn't it?"

He read my company name on the side of the truck out loud and shook his head. "The last time I checked, you didn't even have a driver's license. If you're driving illegally, I'm confiscating your vehicle."

"I'm legal," I lied.

"I'm checking right now." Blaze ran back to his truck, yanked the door open, and reached for the radio.

"Blaze," Big Donny called. "We have more important things to do right now. Tell her."

"Tell me what?" I asked, searching their faces. Big Donny looked like he'd swallowed rat poison, his face pasty white like dough, the lines of his mouth twitching.

"Is it about Little Donny? Have you found him?"

"Warrant's been issued for Little Donny's arrest," he said grimly.

We gasped. Cora Mae's was the loudest. Kitty flung her Amazon arms into the air and howled like a gust of forty-mile-an-hour wind.

"WHAT?" I shouted at Blaze.

"His fingerprints were the only ones found on the rifle," Blaze continued. "His footprints were everywhere. Pa's cap was found in the brush near Billy Lundberg . . ."

"Orange cap with Budweiser across the front?" I asked, fear eating at my stomach. "Barney's old cap?"

Blaze nodded. "Carl said he was wearing it."

"Doesn't seem like much evidence against him," I said. "Fingerprints on his own rifle,

95

footprints at his own bait pile, and a cap in the woods. Seems to me you're reacting too hasty."

"And his fingerprints were all over the two arrows they pulled out of Billy Lundberg's back."

Six

"Carl," I said over coffee at his house, "I have to ask you a few questions."

"Go right ahead. If it helps git Little Donny out of this mess, I'm willing."

I pretended to sip my coffee. If I drank one more cup of coffee, my knees would go and I wouldn't be able to climb into my truck. I noticed my hand holding the cup was shaking from large doses of caffeine. I set the cup down.

If it's true that you can tell someone's honest by the look in his eyes, you'd have a hard time pinning Carl's eyes down to study them. They shifted around the room, left and right, up and down, and never rested on my face once. But that's Carl.

He swung his head to the right of where I sat and scratched his chin.

I pulled a notepad out of my jacket and asked the first question. "Did you know that dead agent?"

"Nope."

"What do you think he was doing there?"

Carl shrugged.

"Maybe you were mixed up in something you shouldn't have been in and didn't know it."

"Nope."

"Were those your arrows they pulled out of Billy?"

Carl nodded. "Yep. Blaze showed them to me after I realized mine were missing from our stake-out."

"Was Little Donny fooling with them?"

Carl shrugged.

We sat through a long pause. I watched my hands do the caffeinated jumping bean tap and Carl studied the ceiling. I waited to see if Carl might pick up the conversation on his own.

I couldn't think of anything else to ask him and he wasn't volunteering. I shoved back in my chair.

"I have one question for you, Gertie."

"Okay," I said.

"Blaze told me they found that warden's vehicle parked at the DNR office in Marquette. How'd he git to my pile?"

My mouth fell open. Carl finally looked me full in the eyes with a smug smile. He'd one-upped me and felt pretty good about it.

This was another example of how much I have to learn about my new career. I'd never admit it out loud, but sometimes I act like a real rookie.

What else had I overlooked?

"That's the second Mitch Movers truck I've seen today," Kitty said as she ripped down Highway M35 driving the Trouble Buster. The morning sun zapped through the windshield and bounced against my Blublocker sunglasses. "Seems like everybody's moving."

She had the gleam in her eye that she gets when she's driving. Ordinarily I won't ride in a car Kitty is driving, because she gets insane the minute she slides behind the wheel, but circumstances forced me into a tight spot.

"Blaze just drove by in his sheriff's truck," Cora Mae had said when we pulled into Kitty's yard. "And he parked right up the road. You can see a speck of his truck through the pines over there."

I glanced in the direction of the road, squinting through the trees. Sure enough, there he was. "Well, trade places with me. Quick."

"I don't have a license either."

"I forgot that," I said, rolling down the

window when Kitty thundered down the steps from her house. "Come around this side." I motioned to Kitty and slid to the middle of the truck. "You're going to have to drive us out of here. Blaze is after me."

And that's how she got behind the wheel. We waved to Blaze as we drove by and he pulled out and stayed with us till we were well out of Stonely.

"Pull over," I said when he finally turned off. "He's gone now."

I felt the truck's acceleration. Cora Mae and I clutched the dashboard and both of us stomped on an imaginary brake.

"No, he's not," Kitty said. "I just caught a glimpse of him and you know how duplicitous he can be."

"He can't be back there, or he'd have pulled you over by now for speeding and reckless endangerment of innocent passengers. Enough of this rigamarole."

Rigamarole was the biggest word I could come up with to counter Kitty's *duplicitous,* considering the kind of pressure I was under.

Kitty made a right turn on two wheels.

"Holy cripes," Cora Mae said, which is the closest she ever comes to swearing.

I pulled my stun gun out of my purse and threatened to use it on Kitty.

100

"You wouldn't," she said.

"Try me," I said, turning it on.

And that's how I got my truck back.

I drove down the bluff, around the outskirts of Gladstone, past the train station, along Lake Michigan, and crossed the bridge over the Escanaba River as it flows into Escanaba.

Kitty guided me through the big-city traffic and pointed out a parking space across from St. Francis Hospital on Ludington Street.

"I'm waiting in the truck," Cora Mae announced. "This is too creepy for me."

"No way," I said. "An investigator can't wait it out in the car anytime things get messy."

"I can't do it," Cora Mae insisted.

"You go on ahead, Kitty. We'll be right behind you."

"Don't take too long," Kitty called. "You have all the questions in your little notebook."

Kitty had already tracked down her source by the time Cora Mae worked up the courage to enter the building.

"Johnny here is going to help us," she said, pointing at a thin, hairless man holding a broom. The janitor. Just great. I needed a medical analysis on two dead bodies and Kitty gets a janitor to help us.

"Hey, Kit," he said with a big smile. "Come on back."

We followed him down a long, narrow hallway, rode the elevator to the basement, and turned into a room that smelled of disinfectants.

"Want to see the bodies?" One eye winked at Kitty.

She looked at me. I wondered if they were naked and had been stitched up after the autopsies or if their insides were in a bag somewhere leaving body cavities exposed.

I shook my head, clutching Cora Mae's arm so she couldn't escape. "That won't be necessary. Just tell us what the medical examiner learned."

"Well," he leaned closer in a conspiratorial gesture, the fluorescent lights of the morgue reflecting off his scalp. "One had his head blown off and the other one's lungs were punctured by arrows."

I looked at the janitor. "We already know that."

"Well that's the whole thing then," he said, slapping his hands together. "I can't tell you anymore."

I glared at Kitty. I could be searching the woods for Little Donny instead of wasting my time here.

"Might be something you could use in his belongings," he said, watching Kitty.

Now you're talking, I thought.

"But I could get in a whole lot of trouble. If you know what I mean."

Kitty, pin-curls and all, weighing three times more than Johnny, licked her lips. "I'll make it worth your while."

Cora Mae and I slipped to the other side of the room while negotiations continued between Kitty and Johnny. A few minutes later, Kitty waved us over.

I already knew what Billy Lundberg had with him because Cora Mae and I had searched his pockets in the woods. So I went right to the warden's bag, and I pulled out his clothes and shoes and glanced at the items that had been removed from his pockets. Nothing unusual.

I picked up his shoes and turned them over. Noticing a small downy feather embedded in the deep crevices of one of the soles, I carefully pulled it out.

"A baby bird feather," Kitty whispered in case I didn't know what it was.

Kitty's janitor friend guarded the door, making sure no one was coming down the hall, so I slipped the feather into my pocket. My first possible clue, I thought, grasping for straws, or in this case, feathers.

Coming out of the building, I sucked in deep breaths of fresh air, grateful to be alive and well.

I'd never been to the motor vehicle department before, so I wasn't prepared for the foul dispositions I encountered. According to Kitty, they're always like that.

I was treated less than subhuman, and if I ever run into that woman in a dark alley, watch out.

"You can't just have a license," she snorted with disdain. "You need a vision test, a written test, and then you get your temporary license. If you pass. After that, you take a road test."

"I'm ready for the first step," I said. "Kitty, stay close by, I might need help."

"If you cheat, you have to wait six months before you can try again," said Miss Foul Personality.

Kitty moved off into the waiting area.

I passed the vision test with flying shapes and colors. The written test was the problem.

After looking over the questions I asked the woman, "How am I supposed to know all this stuff?"

"Didn't you read the booklet?"

"The booklet? Oh, never mind. I back-seat drove for Barney for forty-some years. I can pass this test." I filled it out and handed it in as if I was still in grade school.

"You failed the test," she said, throwing a booklet in my general direction.

When we were back in the truck, Cora Mae hooted, "I can't believe you failed the test for your temps. That's the easiest part." Hee, hee, haw, haw.

"It was the signs," I said, putting on my directional to turn toward Stonely. "Those shapes are very confusing. I don't know how Lead-Foot Kitty managed to pass."

"I'm a good driver," Kitty said. "I can teach you because when you finally manage to get your temps, you can't drive alone."

"What do you mean?"

"You have to have someone with a permanent license in the car with you."

The rules the government manages to come up with! "I wouldn't have to do this in the first place if Blaze would pay attention to his job and leave me alone. His priorities are mixed up."

I dropped my partners at their homes and pulled into my driveway.

Detective No-Neck Sheedlo was still planted in a car on the side of the house, but I didn't see the savage tracking dog.

Star had offered to entertain Heather, Big Donny, and Grandma Johnson at her house for the afternoon, so I had my place to myself for a few hours.

I pulled out a police catalog I'd snitched from Blaze's house last time I visited. Using my credit card, I called in an order and requested overnight delivery.

"A detective badge," I said into the phone, noticing they weren't cheap. "And a voice-activated micro-recorder."

For the first time in days I took a nap on the couch. When I woke up, I rubbed my neck and realized I was still sitting up. That's one thing I seem to be doing more and more. Sleeping upright is becoming easier.

I spent the rest of the afternoon in the woods looking for Little Donny, walking down deer trails leading away from Carl's bait pile, stopping once in a while and calling out his name. I followed trail after trail, calling and calling until my voice became hoarse and my legs grew heavy and weak.

Little Donny had been missing since Monday. Lost without food or water or shelter for three days. How long could he last? Was he still alive?

"How can you sit here stuffing your face

with scrambled eggs when Little Donny might be . . ." I hesitated and glanced at Heather and Big Donny, who were staring back at me with wide, terrified eyes. "Hungry too," I added.

"Now, Ma," Blaze answered. "We're doing everything we can to find him. Didn't you see the planes going over? We're searching on the ground and from the sky. What else can we do?"

"I suppose you're using that poor excuse for a tracking dog?"

"Deputy Snell is retiring him. After he confused you twice with Little Donny, he decided to put him out to pasture."

"Where's he going?" I wanted to know.

Blaze shrugged.

I felt bad. Fred had been fired for incompetence, and a certain portion of it was my fault. He'd done the right thing chasing me around, but no one else knew it, and I wasn't about to inform them.

Grandma Johnson shuffled out of her room, her black hairnet pulled down over her brow and her new teeth clacking. She proceeded to make a fresh pot of coffee, forgetting to add the ground coffee beans to the filter. But we've all done that.

Heather slumped on the couch with large dark circles under her eyes, adding a damp crumpled tissue to the pile scattered on the end table.

"Little Donny didn't do it," she said, a chant we'd heard several times in the last few minutes.

"Of course not," I said. Again.

"Deputy Snell wants all the family members to go down and get fingerprinted," Blaze said. "Unless your prints are already on file. I think it's a good idea."

"I'm a stockbroker," Big Donny puffed. "Mine are already on file."

"Heather, you and Ma have to go down."

"Why would Deputy Dickey think we have to do that?" I demanded.

"Seems there were unidentifiable prints in Little Donny's car. He just wants to clear up a few details, and if he has your prints, it'll help. And he doesn't like to be called Deputy Dickey. We've been over that before. His name is Deputy Snell."

I thought about my prints all over Little Donny's car, which wasn't a big deal, but this was clearly an infringement of my privacy. I thought about superglue. If I dried it on my fingers, would it alter my prints?

I decided I wouldn't cooperate. Let Deputy Dickey arrest me.

"Why don't you bring me that dog," I said to Blaze. "I've been thinking about getting one for a while. He'd do fine."

The entire family stared at me, including Grandma Johnson, who almost dropped her uppers into the coffee pot.

"There isn't room for him in the truck," Cora Mae complained when she saw Fred sitting next to me. He had already slobbered up the passenger side window and was working on the front window. Long, wet, sliding nose and tongue drool oozed and began drying in streaks. I'd have to start carrying paper towels in the truck.

His tail pounded against the seat as he checked out Cora Mae, nudging her with his nose. She shrunk away, intimidated by his black bulk and red devil eyes. After spending a few hours with him she would figure out, just as I had, that he's a harmless baby underneath his fierce exterior.

"He looks like a killer. Vicious, mean, and look at those teeth."

"He and I didn't have a very good start," I said. "But, in this case, first appearances don't count. He isn't working right now, so he's a lamb. Once he's on the job, he takes it very seriously."

"What's this?" Cora Mae held up a canning jar filled with water.

"That's Fred's travel mug."

"How's Kitty going to fit?" she said, scrunching up against the door.

"She's not coming along today," I said, dodging Fred's tail. Kitty barely fit in the truck with just Cora Mae and me. With Fred, no way. "But she gave me directions."

We rattled down a gravel road with craters the size of basketballs scattered across it. I weaved through, trying to miss the holes.

Ernie Pelto was out back of his house in an open field, watching the sky. As Cora Mae and I walked out to join him, I could hear Fred crying. It had been a struggle just to get out of the truck without him, and now he was making such a racket he could be heard in the next town.

"I was expecting you," Ernie said. "Kitty called."

He wore a thick glove on his right hand. "Stand back," he warned us.

A large hawk flew toward us and landed gracefully on his raised arm. He smiled and rubbed the bird's back.

We followed Ernie and the bird to the house, where the hawk hopped to a perch. Ernie, a big, round Finn with an easy grin, removed the glove.

I held out the feather I had found on the dead warden's shoe, my one and only clue.

Ernie studied it. "A brancher," he said.

"Probably a red-tailed hawk. It hasn't molted into its adult plumage yet."

"A brancher?" I asked, aware that I was revealing my lack of worldly experience to my business partner, Cora Mae.

"A brancher is a young hawk," Ernie explained. "We like to get them young and raise them ourselves. This is a young one."

"Where would the warden have picked up this feather?" I wanted to know. "It was on the bottom of his shoe, in the creases."

"Wasn't likely he ran across it in the woods, although it's possible. Walking through a field maybe, since he was a warden and they go all over." Ernie looked doubtful.

"But . . . ?" I prompted.

"When was the last time you had a feather stuck to your shoe after coming out of the woods?"

I thought about that. "Never."

"When was the last time you had a feather stuck on your shoe from walking through a field?"

"Never." I glanced at Cora Mae. "How about you, Cora Mae?"

"Can't remember ever having a feather stuck to my shoe, or walking through a field — except now."

The three of us eyed her black spike heels.

"But go into a chicken coop," Ernie said. "And you'll have them on there for sure. Same with this feather. He might have been visiting a falconer with a lot of birds. There are a few of us around."

I knew a little about hawking. You have to apply for a license to own a raptor, and a license isn't easy to get. It required a long apprenticeship under a licensed sponsor. I also knew that, to protect the birds, there were strict rules about capturing them.

Cora Mae studied Ernie, and I could tell she was sizing him up for future consideration in the Cora Mae broken-heart club.

He reached up and scratched his face and a wedding ring on his finger caught the gleam of the sun.

"I'll meet you back at the car," said Cora Mae, my relentless investigator, after seeing the flash. She sashayed away.

"Any wardens been around here lately?" I asked.

"No, it's been awhile."

"I'm trying to find out about that warden who was murdered over by Stonely." I held up the feather again. "This is my only clue."

"Not much of a clue."

"It's all I have."

"The DNR has a list of all the local falconers. You could start there."

SEVEN

Cora Mae and Kitty offered to comb the woods for Little Donny to give me a break. I chuckled to Fred, sitting in the passenger seat of my new yellow truck. I pictured Cora Mae on her spiky heels and hefty Kitty crashing through the woods. At least I'd dressed them up in hunter's orange so no one would mistake them for bears.

I hoped I wouldn't have two more people to search for when I got back.

"We might as well drive into Marquette for the list of falconers and kill two birds with one stone," I said to my canine friend, Fred. "We'll get the list of falconers and maybe find out why the warden was this far south."

I was going to like Fred, despite his slobber on my window. He was the only one in the bunch that didn't argue with me every time I opened my mouth.

I'd pawned Heather and Big Donny off

on Blaze and Grandma Johnson, leaving me free to investigate. I grimaced when I remembered the family meal coming up tonight at my house, hoping I'd have good news.

Little Donny couldn't possibly be lost in the woods anymore, and that really worried me. By now, he would have stumbled onto a road, eventually leading him safely to food and shelter. Even though the forests are vast in the U.P., it's not like being lost in northern Canada.

No, either Little Donny was in hiding, or something was preventing him from coming out.

I backed out of my driveway into the narrow road that runs past my place. Carl in his station wagon had been about to cruise by, but slowed and stopped behind me, waiting for me to drive off. Instead, I hopped down and walked back to his car.

Carl rolled down his window about half an inch. His eyes bobbed up and down and settled on his windshield.

"Anything new on Little Donny?" he asked.

I shook my head. "Seems the whole county's looking for him. Sheriff's vehicles everywhere, helicopters and small planes flying over. You'd think someone would know something. Want to come over for a family get-together tonight? George will be there."

Carl glanced at a covered dish on the seat next to him. "Thanks for the offer, but me and some of the boys are playing poker. We're all bringin' a dish to pass."

Traffic began backing up behind us. Hardly anyone uses the side road where I live, but just stop to chat and everybody around has to come along and bother you.

A small white van with "Mitch Movers" stenciled on its side idled behind Carl. The driver revved the engine and drove around without so much as a glance our way. I waved to Betty Berg, next in the line-up, and headed back to my truck.

Fred greeted me from the passenger seat like I'd been gone a week.

Marquette is straight north from Stonely about an hour's drive. I followed Highway M35 past Sawyer Air Force Base, where in August you can pick blueberries the size of Concord grapes.

The city of Marquette is ringed by tall pines and granite bluffs overlooking Lake Superior. Unlike Escanaba, which lies on the shore of Lake Michigan and has sandy beaches, Marquette was settled on solid rock and rises above the largest of the Great Lakes. The city is large enough for a state prison and Northern Michigan University; it's one of the U.P.'s major metropolises.

A recruitment poster on the door of the DNR office said, "Become a Conservation Officer — Protect our great outdoors."

A young man with a starched and pressed uniform and polished shoes greeted me.

"I'm investigating the murder of Robert Hendricks," I said, thinking about flashing my new detective badge, which had arrived on my porch right on schedule. I rejected the idea as premature but had my new voice-activated micro-recorder turned on in my purse.

I noticed Warden Burnett standing at a file cabinet. He looked up. "What authority do you have to b-b-be asking questions about Warden Hendricks?"

"I'm investigating at the family's request," I lied, suspecting he'd follow up if I tried the detective routine. "Don't you remember me? We met the other day at the scene."

"We've already t-told the sheriff everything we know." He walked toward me, his expression softening only slightly.

"I wanted to know what he was doing so far south," I said. "Rolly Akkala is our local warden and I thought he handled everything in the Stonely area."

"Stonely's within the district Hendricks was assigned to," Burnett said, frowning and speaking very slowly. I noticed that the stutter vanished when he concentrated on pronunciation. "What are you implying?"

"Just seems strange to me. The only warden I know is Rolly. I heard your warden's car was back here in Marquette. How did he get to that bait pile where he was killed?"

"We use all k-kinds of t-transportation, as I already explained to the sheriff. He might have been d-driving an ATV."

"All the way from Marquette?"

"That part's not clear yet," he admitted, slapping a file folder against the palm of his hand.

"Any of your vehicles missing?"

"As a m-matter of fact, one of our ATVs is missing."

"Really," I said, surprised. "No one's mentioned that to me."

"We just realized it was gone. And you aren't on my l-list of people to contact."

"Better notify the sheriff's office. Maybe they can trace it." I dug a freshly printed business card out of my purse and handed it to him. "If you remember anything else, please call me. I'm helping the family."

He tucked it in his shirt pocket without looking at it.

"Oh," I said, remembering the second item on my agenda. "I'd like to know what falconers live between here and Stonely."

"Falconers?"

"You know, those guys that fly hawks and falcons from their arms."

"I know what a falconer is. Any p-particular reason?"

"No, just thought I could find a sponsor. I'm thinking about going into it."

Warden Burnett stared at me from under hooded eyes. "I'll g-get someone to help you," he said, walking off. I hung around in the front office until a woman from the clerical staff presented me with a print-out.

When I left the building I turned off my new micro-recorder.

A lot of arguing goes on about the origin of pasties. For those unfamiliar with pasties, they have nothing to do with costumes worn by women in sleazy stripper bars. They are meat pies.

The Finns and Swedes like to think they created pasties, and they have an ongoing dispute with another ethnic group that makes the same claim. The Cornish say their miners brought them to the U.P. in the 1800s when the copper mines opened up. I don't really know who's right.

During deer hunting season in November, the Senior Citizens group makes the best I've ever had, but mine are close.

I finished rolling out the dough in plate-sized rounds, added ground meat, potatoes, onions, salt, pepper, and, of course, my special secret ingredient. I've been experimenting in case I ever get to write that U.P. cookbook I've been thinking about for so long.

I popped the pasties into the oven as George walked in the door. His snake hat coiled from its position under his arm and I could see he'd slicked down his hair for this special visit.

"Haven't seen much of you lately," he said, eyeing Fred, who sat at attention playing sentinel at the door. Only the brave would pass without permission. George scratched Fred's ear and Fred rubbed his large head against George's leg.

"My new tracking dog," I said with pride. Fred was turning out to be very well trained and he hadn't chewed anything up yet.

"Scary-looking."

"I thought you might cancel for the poker game tonight. I'm glad you came."

"What poker game?" George wanted to know.

"The one Carl's at."

"Hum, no one mentioned a poker game to me."

"Well, maybe you don't know everything that goes on."

George shrugged and plopped into my rocking chair. George is a rocker, spending hours at it if he has time. Today there was just enough time for me to fill him in on my trip to Marquette before the rest of the family began to arrive.

Heather and Big Donny slumped out of the guest bedroom, blinking like moles creeping out of the ground to discover sunlight for the first time.

"Finally get some sleep?" I asked.

"Those sleeping pills Blaze got for us from the doctor really work," Heather said, yawning.

Blaze puffed in, still wearing his sheriff's uniform and eyed up the oven.

"Mary isn't feeling too good," he said. "She decided to stay home rather than risk giving Grandma Johnson the flu. Star has a big date and isn't coming either."

"Time for someone to knock on Grandma Johnson's bedroom door and tell her nap-time is over," I said, taking the cookie sheets

120

filled with pasties out of the oven.

No one moved.

"Big Donny," I said, "go get Grandma."

He groaned and went down the hall.

"Donny's going home in the morning," Heather said, as everyone sat down at the table except Grandma. I walked around the table dishing out steaming pasties. "He has to get back to the office, and this sitting around waiting is slowly killing him. But I'm staying as long as it takes."

"Once we find Little Donny, it's only a five-hour drive to get back," I said, relieved because Big Donny makes me nervous.

Heather burst out crying. "I keep thinking this is a bad dream, and I'll wake up. But I don't. Once they find him, he won't be able to come home, will he?"

"No." Blaze shook his head. "He won't."

"What are these things?" Big Donny said, eyeing up his dinner. "Some sort of Yooper pot pie?"

"They have these in the supermarkets back home," Heather said, none too politely, and I knew the stress was really getting to her. "Just eat it."

I squeezed her shoulders. "Don't worry. I'm on the case and I'll find the real killer."

Blaze glared at me. "Deputy Snell and Deputy Sheedlo are doing a fine job under

121

my direction. You can butt out, Ma."

"You already have Little Donny tried and convicted. You're his uncle and you're not doing a thing to clear him."

Grandma Johnson shuffled to the table and made a big deal of pulling out her chair.

"You done it again," she crabbed. "All bellied up to the table before you come and git me."

There was a perfectly good reason for that, and it was because Grandma Johnson dishes dirt. Ninety-two years old and a regular spitfire.

"I called you to the table," Big Donny said. "Don't you remember?"

"Something's funny-tasting about these pasties," she said, ignoring Big Donny and digging in like she hadn't eaten for a week.

By the silence around the table, I knew she was alone in her assessment. Everyone scooped chunks of potatoes and meat into their mouths, contentment spreading across their faces. Even Big Donny looked satisfied once he got past his initial forkful.

George squirted ketchup on his pasty. "What does Rolly Akkala say about the dead warden?"

I paused with my fork halfway to my mouth.

I hadn't thought to talk to him. Rolly was

the local laughingstock. There were more stories about Rolly's wardening skills than there were Polish and dumb blonde jokes.

Rolly's been known to lie down in front of vehicles so his alleged hunting violators can't drive off. He says he has a dangerous job, but I say he makes it that way with his own stupidity. One day he'll become road kill, crushed under the tire of someone who's had his fill of the government.

I'd have to talk to him.

Blaze removed his fork from his mouth and shifted pasty to the side of his cheek. "Rolly doesn't know a thing."

"And that crazed dog by the door," Grandma Johnson said sharply. "Wouldn't be surprised if it kills us all. Barney's turning over in his grave for sure. I'm afraid to come down the hall, it's got so bad. Pretty soon I won't be able to leave my bedroom." Her teeth snapped and she glared my way.

That, I didn't dare inform her, was my plan.

I'm not sure I slept at all. Tossing and turning, I watched the alarm clock roll through the early hours of the morning. Two o'clock, three, four-fifteen. At five I pulled my sixty-six-year-old body from bed, my muscles stiff and bunched from stress, with the taste of fear in my mouth.

On this frost-covered dawn morning, I faced the possibility that something awful and unspeakable had happened to Little Donny. With the entire Upper Peninsula searching, how could he still be missing? If he was alive without shelter, last night's freeze would have killed him. When last I'd seen him he was dressed for hunting in the warmth of the day, not for overnight camping. And what about food? Little Donny couldn't make it an hour and a half without filling up, let alone four days.

I huddled over my cup of coffee as the sun rose over the east field, wondering where to turn next. Fred stretched out at my feet, and I buried my toes in the warmth of his coat, my usually optimistic mind filled with serious doubt.

"I got the job," I said into the phone.

"What job?" Cora Mae asked.

"Remember," I said, impatient from lack of sleep. "The census taker job I applied for last month."

My first job application and interview in over thirty years and I'd landed it. It was only a temporary position but it would bring in a little cash to supplement my Social Security.

"Aren't you a little busy to take on a new job?" Cora Mae said.

"No, no, this is perfect timing. I can get inside people's homes and question them about Little Donny. This gives me carte blanche to handle the investigation any way I want to."

"When do you start?"

"Today. A trainer's coming right to my house to get me started with the paperwork. She'll be here any minute."

Rolly Akkala liked to cover his tracks. As our local game warden he managed to rile a lot of people who grew up with weapons, so he kept on the move and changed his routine often. Nobody had been able to find out where he lived, but a few locals had worked for years to discover that pertinent bit of information.

He wouldn't be easy to track down without help.

The Deer Horn Restaurant was my first stop. Fred howled from the passenger seat as soon as I opened the door to the restaurant. Ruthie, frazzled as usual because she couldn't keep good help and did most of the work alone, managed to function as hostess, waitress, and supervisor of the cooking help when she lucked out and found someone who could actually cook. Otherwise she did that, too.

"Be right with you, Gertie," she said, trotting for the kitchen.

"Just a cup of coffee when you have a spare minute," I called after her and took a stool at the counter.

"What's that noise outside?" someone asked.

"Sounds like a coyote or a wolf," someone else said.

"In broad daylight? They sure are getting bold."

I didn't say a word, knowing the howling would soon die down, like it usually did when Fred lost sight of me long enough.

"I'm looking for Rolly," I said to Otis Knutson, who spends his life driving freight trains up and down the tracks. Occasionally he stops the train on Stonely's tracks for a quick bite and to catch up on the local gossip. He sat at the counter next to Carl. Both were munching on the daily special, meatloaf and mashed potatoes.

Otis chuckled. "Last I heard he was letting the air out of one of those out-of-stater's tires to slow him down for questioning. He's fiddling with the valve and while he's doin' that the guy gets in his car, doesn't even know Rolly's crouched down back there, and he throws it in reverse, runnin' right over Rolly's foot. Crushed all the bones. Rolly's limpin' around somethin' awful."

Carl laughed until he began to snort, even though I'm sure he'd heard the story more than once. "Last I heard he set up a roadblock over on Rock Road and he's checking for violators. He's already arrested some goof dragging a buck out of the brush. The fella said it looked like a bear to him when he shot it, but on closer inspection he realized it was a deer and he was draggin' it out to report it."

We all knew how dumb city people could be. "Sounds reasonable to me," I said.

"Only mistake the guy made was he had it all gutted out and ready to hang. And it had a rack on it the size of a young tamarack tree. Would'a been hard to mistake for a bear."

Ruthie poured coffee all around and whisked off.

"Any word on Little Donny?" Otis asked, scraping the last of the potatoes into his mouth.

I shook my head. "No. I don't know what to think anymore. Blaze works twenty-four hours a day, organizing search parties. They've trampled the woods for miles in every direction and the boy's not showing up. Heather hasn't heard a word. You'd think he'd call her if he's okay . . ."

"He'll turn up sooner or later," Carl said and stood up. Ruthie brought him a carry-out bag. He picked up his check and slowly counted out a few bills.

I eyed the bag and Carl noticed. "Another round of meatloaf for later," he explained. "You know I hate to cook."

After Carl left, Otis said, "It's a good sign, Gertie. If they're combing the woods without finding him, it's a good sign."

"You're right," I agreed. "At least they aren't finding a body."

"Right."

The silence between us grew. Otis picked up his check and fumbled through his back pocket for his wallet.

"Time to find Rolly," I said, draining my coffee and patting Otis on the back. "Anyone know where our local warden's hiding out?"

A few customers gave me ideas, places to start, but no one knew for sure.

I found Rolly's truck parked on the side of Rock Road. After I put Fred on a leash, we walked around the truck while he sniffed away. He caught a scent and hauled me down a deer trail at a faster clip than I was used to. I'd have to teach Fred how to walk on a leash instead of dragging me on my knees or my face. About the time I thought my arm would disconnect from its socket, we found Rolly. He had a hunter cornered in a tree. Or at least that's what I thought at first.

Rolly eyed Fred as we pulled up, and Fred, thrilled that he had his man cornered, pulled off his usual drill by howling and going for a grip on Rolly's pants. I yanked him away at the last second, although I considered letting Fred go about his business. It would have been one small victory over our local government.

"Sit," I said to Fred, and to my amazement he sat. But he didn't take his red devil eyes off of the warden.

Rolly had his hands on his hips, exposing his sidearm. "They find that murdering grandson of yours yet?"

"I thought that was your job. You should be out searching for him instead of running innocent hunters up trees."

We both looked up and so did Fred. The guy was about fifteen feet off the ground.

"He's stuck up there," Rolly said.

"Quit standing there doing nothing," the hunter called out. "Help me down."

The thing that amazed me was that the hunter's aluminum tree stand was in a different tree than he was. He was clutching the side of an enormous oak tree, and his tree stand, or what was left of it, sat in a maple about four feet away. Part of the stand lay in a heap on the ground.

"How'd you get over there?" I asked.

"The bottom part of my tree stand fell to the ground when I was inching up and I got stuck in the maple for the longest time on what was left of it." He had his face plastered against the tree limb and his legs were contorted, one stuck into the crook of a small branch, the other twisted around the enormous tree. "I yelled and yelled, and when nobody came I thought I'd have a better chance of getting down by jumping to this tree."

He chanced a glimpse at a smaller branch five feet below where he was hanging. "I missed," he explained.

"I hate my job," Rolly muttered under his breath.

"Jump," I called. "I think you can make it without breaking anything."

"Are you nuts?" the hunter shouted.

"Shinny down, then," Rolly said. "Go on, clamp your legs around the tree just like

130

you're doing now and bear hug your way down."

With enough encouragement and a final threat of being abandoned in the woods for the night, the hunter managed to climb out of the tree.

"Where you going?" Rolly shouted as the man bolted for the trail. "Get back here and get this tree stand out of my woods, and while you're at it, I'll take a look at your bear license."

After Rolly assured himself that everything was nice and legal, Fred and I followed him to his truck. Rolly had a bulldog's waddle, the result of thick, short legs and a barrel chest. His jaw covered half his head. A pronounced limp reminded me of Otis' story.

"What happened to your leg?"

"Charley horse, is all," Rolly muttered.

"Did you know Warden Hendricks?" I asked when we arrived at the road.

" 'Course I did. We're all like family."

"Why do you think he was shot?"

"Your grandson was up to something illegal, is why."

I gave Rolly a squinty-eyed, stern look. "I'm not going to get into it with you over whether Little Donny did it or not. I'm asking you if you know something that would help."

"Help what?"

"Help me figure this all out and help me find Little Donny."

"We'd all like to find that kid." Rolly opened his truck door and pulled himself in. I wedged my body between him and the door so he couldn't close it.

"I hear Hendricks' vehicle was back in Marquette. How'd he get down here?"

Rolly stuck a key in the ignition but didn't turn it. "Stay out of our business, Gertie. The kid did it and it's that simple."

"If you know so much, you can explain why he is supposed to have also killed Billy Lundberg."

"Sure, I can answer that, but you aren't going to like it. He killed one man and had his first taste of human blood. He's on a rampage and he'll kill again, just you wait and see."

Rolly is perfect for his job — narrow-minded, obsessed with his own book of rules, and a true backwoods fanatic. He doesn't seem to mind that he's ridiculed and reviled all across Tamarack County.

"One more thing," I said. "Tell me about trapping birds."

"What do you mean?"

"Raptors. If I want one for a pet, can I go

132

and trap one?"

"No! No! No!"

I finally had his attention. He gripped the steering wheel and pulled himself around to get a better look at me. "You have to have a special license and to get that you need a sponsor and —"

"Maybe I can buy a bird."

"No! No! No! They're protected and you can't buy them. Get yourself a parrot."

"Can't I buy one from someone around here?"

Rolly sighed and began reciting the rules. "The only people that can have raptors are licensed falconers and they can only have two birds unless they're masters — then they can have three. It's illegal to buy or sell raptors or their eggs. Every bird has a marker around its leg with a federal identification bearing a serial number and if I catch you with one, I'll arrest you."

"Who around here has a bunch of them?"

"I just explained it to you. No one has a bunch of them. It's illegal." Rolly started his truck and I moved away so he could close the door.

"I hate my job," I heard him mutter before the door slammed shut.

EIGHT

Kitty and I were seated at Cora Mae's kitchen table comparing notes and planning the next step in our quest to find Little Donny and the real killer. We were on our third pot of coffee and I'd had my two's-the-limit sugar doughnuts.

The feather decorated the center of the table.

"We sure don't have much," Kitty said, eyeing it.

"If we could trace Hendricks' steps in the last few days of his life, we'd be way ahead of where we are now." I reached for another doughnut. To heck with limits. "But DNR agents run all over the place. He could have been anywhere." I picked up the bird feather. "This feather is my only lead."

"And he doesn't have any family around here at all?" Cora Mae held a minuscule doughnut crumb between two manicured fingernails and touched it to her tongue.

Not an ounce of fat on that woman, but what she goes through to stay that way isn't worth it, in my book.

"A brother in Florida and an ex-wife," I said. "But they divorced twelve years ago."

"Ex-wives can hold a grudge a long time," Cora Mae observed.

"This ex lives out west and her whereabouts have been confirmed by Blaze's storm troopers." I licked sugar from my fingers and watched Kitty polish off her sixth doughnut. "We have to have a lucky break soon."

"Speaking of lucky," Cora Mae said, fluffing her hair. "Kitty and I are double-dating tonight."

I sucked sugar down the wrong pipe and started coughing. Even though Kitty claims she's a big, as in HUGE, hit with the men, this was my first evidence of it. I wondered if she would comb out her pin curls for the guy.

"And we'd like you to go too."

I had tears in my eyes from coughing on doughnut crumbs, or so I pretended. I shook my head violently. It wasn't even two years since Barney died, way too soon for dating, and if I did decide to date again, it wouldn't be a triple date.

"The Detroit boys," Kitty explained.

"Cora Mae's going out with BB, and I'm going out with Marlin. That leaves Remy without a date. How about it?"

"I'm working tonight at my new census job," I explained, with a hint of false disappointment in my voice, grasping frantically for a valid excuse. "Any other time and I'd really like to go along. You two have fun."

"I didn't know you took a night job," Cora Mae whined.

"It's some days and some nights, depending on what area I'm covering."

"You can set your own hours," Cora Mae insisted. "You don't have to work tonight."

"I want to make a good impression."

"We'll miss you," Kitty said, picking up another doughnut.

This new job was already coming in handy for dodging unpleasant social situations.

My job was to visit every household in the town of Stonely as well as the outlying areas, and gather information for the government. I know in the past I've said some pretty harsh things about our government and I'm not taking any of my words back. Now, instead of giving them all my money, they'll be paying some of it back to me.

Our government is run by a bunch of crooks and there's no getting around it. But the job has some interesting aspects that will enhance my private investigator business. For example, I go out whenever I want to — days, nights or weekends — and I interview household members. Besides the information the government requires on its standard form, I can ask away on any subject I want.

I have my own census worker badge, and I think it will get me in the door better than my new detective badge once I start testing it out.

At the first door I said, "You didn't send in your census form." I'd barely completed my sentence before the door slammed shut right in my face. I made a mark on my form the way the trainer taught me.

The second door I knocked on was opened by a large gorilla-like guy wearing a muscle shirt. He let me explain who I was. Then without a word, he started to open the door wider, and I thought I was being welcomed in. Instead, a Doberman the size of Detroit passed through the widening opening and made straight for me. The dog ran me off, snarling and barking at my heels.

I put another mark on my form with a huge exclamation point and decided to discuss dogs with my trainer, since she hadn't mentioned one word about them as potential problems. I wasn't trying this one again without Fred as backup.

Jackie Hoholik lived in the next house on my list. She'd been raised by old man Gus, a Finn from the old school. He had a Finnish accent, even though he'd been born and raised in the United States. He must have picked it up from his parents, who immigrated to America in the early 1900s and settled in Calumet.

Jackie was the oldest of Gus' six girls and he brought her up as though she was a boy. Stockily built with short dark hair, she could shoot an acorn off a stump from across a field. She wins every shooting contest in Tamarack County and keeps the men hopping, trying to outdo her.

She hunts every animal in every season and always bags her limit. And I hear she can drink everyone at Herb's Bar under the table.

"Hey, Gert," she said, studying my census badge and opening the door wide. "Come on in."

"I'm working today, Jackie," I said just to warn her. "This is a business call."

"I can see that."

"You didn't send in your census form, so I have to ask you a few questions." I braced for her reaction. If it was anything like the last two, she was about to heave me over her head and throw me out on my backside.

Jackie smiled. "Want a cup of coffee?"

I smiled back with relief. "Sure."

We ran through my questions quickly — how many people live in the house, what are their ages, blah, blah, blah. Since I knew she lived alone, it was an easy interview.

"Sorry about your grandson," she said, refreshing my coffee cup. "Have you found him yet?"

"No. He didn't do it, you know."

"I've known your family my whole life. You're all honest and hard-working. I never knew a Johnson to even steal an apple from a tree. I know he didn't do anything wrong."

"I need to find out where that warden was the day before he died. All I have is this." I pulled the feather out of my purse. "Ernie Pelto, the falconer, says it's a feather from a young red-tail."

I explained where I found the feather and what Ernie told me about where bird feathers stick to shoes. "He says it's unusual for a feather to stick unless you're walking in a whole pile of them, and he says maybe it came from a falconer's place."

She opened her eyes wide and stared at the feather. "I have something to show you," she said.

■ ■ ■ ■

"Put this on." Jackie handed me a helmet.

We were standing out on her cement driveway next to a motorcycle. She slid onto the bike and revved it up. "Hop on."

"It's getting dark," I said, brightly. "Let's do this tomorrow." I'd never been on a motorcycle in my life and I wasn't excited about starting now.

"I think you want to see what I have to show you. It's out by my bear blind. You'll be glad you didn't put it off once you see what I want to show you. Climb on."

I lifted a leg and swung it over the back of the bike like I was heaving myself into a saddle. The helmet felt heavy on my head and I worried about tipping over if I leaned too far out.

Jackie turned on the bike's headlights, and we blew smoke down the dirt road with the G-forces tapping at the helmet and my arms locked around Jackie in a death grip.

"Lean into the turn," Jackie yelled over her shoulder.

She swerved suddenly and we began to bounce down a trail, leaving the road far behind us. After a while, I began to relax and re-evaluate my opinion about bikes.

Instead of parking and walking into her bear blind like everyone else had to do, we zipped along the tiny path and arrived in microseconds.

I lifted a leg over the back, stood, and pulled off the helmet. Jackie was already substituting hers for a headlamp, like miners used to wear. She flipped on its light, illuminating the surrounding woods. Darkness crept at us from the sides and behind.

"I found it over here," she said, leading the way.

We passed her bait pile and walked down a deer trail. She stopped and pointed her headlamp into the brush. Stepping closer I noticed we were at the edge of an open field. Something dark and shadowy loomed ahead.

"What is it?" I asked as we neared.

I was looking at a net attached to poles and shaped into a dome. It must have been five feet in diameter. Mice were running around in the netted bottom, scampering over each other, their eyes glowing red in the artificial light.

"It's a raptor trap," Jackie said. "We're looking at it from the back. Here's how it works — a hawk or falcon flying over the field sees the mice and dives in, triggering those little nooses on the bottom. See them there? The bird's feet get tangled in the nooses and it can't escape."

"Is this legal?"

"As long as you have a license and approval by the DNR, you can trap birds. There's a limit on it, though. Maybe one or two each season and a certain kind."

"Quite a coincidence," I muttered.

"Since you're looking for falconers, maybe this is your guy. I found another one on the other side of the field yesterday."

NINE

The next morning dawned sunny and crisp, with a fine layer of frosty dew covering the grass. The guinea hens cackled around the yard, throwing a collective temper tantrum when I let Fred out. They boxed him in, complaining loudly and pecking at his toes, until he bolted from the circle and howled for help at the door. For a big, scary dog, he sure is a sissy.

Blaze pulled in at nine o'clock with my alarm hens announcing his arrival. He walked in a circle around my new truck, shaking his head and swiping his feet at the hens.

"You need to get rid of those dirty birds," he said when he came in and plopped himself at the table.

"Leave my birds alone." I poured him a cup of coffee.

Blaze hadn't slept well. His eyes were red

and puffy and his face was the color of plaster paste. "This doesn't seem real important in the light of all our other problems," he said. "But I have to remind you not to drive that truck. No driver's license yet, I checked, and you can't just stick Pa's old truck plates on another truck. You have to fill out paperwork to transfer them and submit it at the motor vehicle department."

"I know all that. But I have a hard time dealing with the employees down there. I did make an appointment for my test, though," I lied.

"Well, if you need to go anyplace between then and now, I'll take you or Kitty can drive."

If only he knew I was putting my life in Kitty's plump and racy hands every time I scooted into the passenger seat next to her. I never saw anyone stand a vehicle on end taking a corner like Kitty can.

"Warden in Marquette said an ATV was missing." I refilled my coffee cup.

"What were you doing in Marquette?"

"He's my grandson," I said quietly.

Blaze considered that. "The ATV turned up."

"Where? When?" I perked up.

"About a half mile from Walter Laakso's

place the same day you found Billy. By the road."

"Prints?"

Blaze shook his head. "None."

I frowned in thought. "That still doesn't explain how Hendricks got to Little Donny's bait pile. Walter's place is too far away. Hendricks wouldn't have parked the ATV by the side of the road and walked to the pile."

Blaze pushed back in his chair, drained his coffee, and rose.

"Well, I better get back to it," he said, putting on his sheriff's hat and walking out.

"Is that killer dog loose?" Grandma Johnson called from the other end of the hall.

"Yup," I called back.

"They were in the woods together," I said to Cora Mae as I dodged potholes, heading for Jackie Hoholik's house. I'd left Fred home to keep Grandma busy. "The dead warden and the killer were traveling through the woods together."

"How do you know that?" Cora Mae had on one of her man-killer outfits. She hadn't abandoned the black motif but today she added a tight pink sweater with little black bows all over it. Not exactly surveillance gear, but just try to tell Cora Mae anything.

"They were on the ATV together. It's the only thing that makes sense. And it looks like Walter might be involved because Blaze found the ATV right down the road from his house."

"Was it one of Walter's?" Cora Mae had the truck's visor down and was reapplying her lipstick in the tiny mirror, holding her arm steady and watching for potholes out of one eye.

"No. It belonged to the DNR."

"Maybe," Cora Mae said, "the killer parked a truck near Walter's, unloaded the ATV, and they both took off on it. Then the killer murdered Warden Hendricks, returned to his truck, and escaped."

See. Cora Mae is as sharp as a new knife.

"Why didn't he take the ATV along, Miss Fancy Pants?" I said.

Cora Mae shrugged. "Maybe he didn't have time."

"Makes sense." An open stretch of road lay ahead, so I flipped on the lights and siren. "Still working fine," I said. "George really knows what he's doing."

"I'll say."

I pretended not to hear Cora Mae.

Eventually I said, "I thought you were pre-occupied with BB Smith."

She wiggled into a more comfortable posi-

146

tion. "We went to Escanaba for dinner. You should have come along. Poor Remy tagged along all by himself."

"I hope you didn't forget our new business and your mission. You interrogated them, didn't you?"

"What new business? This *Trouble Buster* thing?"

I glanced over in time to see her roll her eyeballs.

Cora Mae continued while smacking her lips. "What do you think we are? The Mod Squad?"

I hit a pothole dead on just to hear her squeal.

"Your hormones are raging out of control," I said. "And you are forgetting that my grandson is wanted for a murder he didn't commit."

Cora Mae caved at that. "You're right. I'm sorry."

"Well, did you get any useful information from them or not?"

"Nothing significant, but I'll work on BB again tonight."

I wasn't surprised that Cora Mae came away empty-handed, considering the Detroit boys' limited gene pool. Her hands weren't the only things that were empty.

"What are you doing?" Cora Mae wanted

to know when I pulled into Jackie Hoholik's driveway and cut the lights and siren.

Hopping out of the truck, I pointed to the motorcycle. "Jackie's working today but she said we could borrow her bike," I said.

Cora Mae got out, too, and emitted an uncertain chuckle. "Get outta here."

"I told her I knew how to drive one and she offered to let me use it."

"That was a total lie," Cora Mae said. "And Blaze will kill you if he finds out. He'll have you declared insane and I'll be forced to testify on his side."

"There's no other way of getting down the paths." I motioned across the road where the trail began and Cora Mae turned and studied it with her hands on her hips. "Unless we walk." I gazed at her shoes.

"I'm not going," she said.

"You have to go." I fitted a helmet over my head and fiddled with the handlebars, trying to remember what Jackie had done to start it. I was pretty sure there was a kick or two in there somewhere. "This is heavier than I thought it would be," I said, surprised when the motor finally fired up. "Help me hold it up."

It was a good thing Little Donny had brought his motor scooter with him last year for me to try out or I never would have figured out how to start the thing.

"I'm not going," Cora Mae repeated while trying to steady the bike, and from the determined look on her face, I suspected I risked losing this round.

"There are two traps set on opposite sides of a wide field," I said. "I can't watch both of them by myself." I played my trump card. "Don't you want to help Little Donny?"

Cora Mae locked eyes with me and I could tell she was studying her options. "How do I get on?" she finally said, grabbing the helmet I held out.

To be honest, I didn't know how I was going to hold up both the bike and Cora Mae, but if Jackie could do it, so could I.

"Keep alert," I said. "You have to help me hold it up with your feet."

The ride began a little wobbly and with a lot of fancy footwork by both of us.

Jackie's next-door neighbor, the gorilla man, came out his front door with his Doberman, and the two of them watched us fly by. I rounded the corner leading down the trail, thankful for the helmet that acted as a disguise. I managed not to tip over even with Cora Mae screaming in my ear.

The trail narrowed as we whizzed along, and I worked the brake to slow us down when we hit the deer path.

"You can't get through here," Cora Mae screamed.

"We did it last night," I called back, but my voice was muffled by the helmet and the roar of the engine. I doubt she heard me.

Tree branches slapped hard against the helmet and Cora Mae's arms tightened around my waist until I thought my eyes would bulge right out. So when I pulled up next to Jackie's blind, I grinned to myself.

Made it.

Now for the stake-out.

"You can stay in the bear stand and watch the first trap from there," I said, shutting off the engine and hanging my helmet on the handlebars, like I've seen real bikers do. "I'll cross the field and watch the other one."

Cora Mae's eyes climbed the tree until they found the stand. "I think you have that mixed up," she said. "I'm going to the other side of the field."

"Suit yourself."

Jackie had laid out a neat little pile of rotting carp for her bears to snack on. By the stack of fish bones next to it, her stop was a popular bear destination.

I rummaged in my weapons purse and extracted two pairs of binoculars, handing one pair to Cora Mae. "If you see anything, just lay low and watch. Here's a radio."

My new two-way radios, another business expense, were about to be put into action for the first time. "Don't use it unless you have to."

I walked her to the edge of the field, gave her directions to the second trap, and watched her stumble through the high grasses, attempting to use her arms like sickles.

By the time I decided she was not going to make it on her own and I'd caught up to her, she'd managed to break a heel and had to be helped across to the trap.

"Right here looks good," I said, breaking loose from her grip on my shoulder and planting her on a log. "Next time, you have to wear hiking boots."

"I don't own anything like . . ." Cora Mae stopped and listened.

I heard it, too.

A car passing nearby.

"There's a road right on the other side of these trees," Cora Mae griped. "We could have driven the truck right up and parked alongside the road instead of almost dying on that motorcycle."

We heard another car pass by.

"But then . . . ," I said, making it up as I went along, hoping to recover from a potentially embarrassing situation, "the trapper

151

might have seen our truck and driven right past. You stay here and pay attention."

"Tell me again why we care about birds?"

"Our only lead is a feather. We have to find out where Warden Hendricks was before he died because he was around birds."

"We need to read up on this detective business. I never expected to be out in the middle of God's country with a broken heel and bugs everywhere."

Cora Mae said "God's country" like it was a dirty word.

I tromped back to my stake-out and studied the tree stand. Jackie had pounded little steps into the tree so I started climbing, my weapons purse slung over my shoulder weighing me down. The platform, once I reached it and figured out how to turn around and scoot my behind onto it, wasn't nearly as big as I thought it would be. It was about the size of the chopping board I use when I make pasties.

As long as I didn't move around much, I wouldn't fall off.

I raised my binoculars and scoped out the falcon trap out in the field. I had a perfect view from the treetop. Perfect enough to see that something was trapped in the netting. Something larger than a mouse.

I was busy watching the snared bird trying to get out of the trap, while I also kept watch across the field for signs of the trapper. I couldn't see Cora Mae from my position.

I dug through my purse and found the two-way radio to check in with Cora Mae, but it slipped out of my fingers and landed at the base of the tree. I looked down and decided to leave it there.

That's when I saw the black bear.

He lazy-shuffled into the clearing and pounced on the bear bait pile right under my dangling feet. He must have weighed five hundred pounds, all rolling six feet of him.

I went over my bear statistics while he sniffed around and grabbed a carp from the hors d'oeuvre tray.

Bears are nearsighted.

That's a good thing.

They can outrun a horse.

Who cares? I didn't plan on a footrace.

They are very good climbers.

Gulp.

I looked around for a baby bear, which would have meant the end for me. No baby. Good. I hadn't expected to see one anyway, because this was no over-protective mean mama. No female would be this enormous.

The bear sat up and snorted the air. I tried hard to hold my breath so I wouldn't emit any human odor.

The pile of bones grew while I took tiny breaths of air.

After a while he lazed over to the bushes and finished off his dinner with a mittful of gooseberries. Then he looked up and saw me.

We faced off. Sort of. He craned his neck in my direction for a better look, then he got up on his hind legs and stretched out, tall and muscular and scary.

I've heard that when a bear is on the defensive, it pops its jaw in a series of rapid snaps as a prelude to a charge.

The bear stared at me and popped his jaw and lips.

At that moment, when I thought I was chopped liver, the radio lying at the base of the tree started crackling and squawking.

The bear didn't hesitate. He took off into the back woods at a dead gallop.

"He's coming your way," Cora Mae's voice shrieked over the airwaves. "Get ready."

She wasn't talking about the bear.

TEN

I watched him come across the open field and head directly for the trap. I fiddled with the adjustments on the binoculars until they sighted in clear and true.

I would have recognized that bulldog waddle even without the advantage of magnification. Along with the limp he'd earned from his encounter with the car tire, our local game warden stood out like a woodchuck lumbering across a lawn.

Rolly Akkala stopped at the trap. He dug into his bag, pulled out a pair of thick gloves, and put them on.

I'd like to say I sailed smoothly down the tree. It was more of a backward dangle from the tree stand while feeling desperately for the first step with my toes, panic building when it didn't present itself. After some terrifying moments I found my foothold and hugged my way down.

Rolly was in the battle of his life by the

time I arrived at the trap.

Cooper's hawks are only medium-sized, but they don't stand down to anything, including a measly game warden. They like to squeeze their prey to death between some of the strongest and most razor-sharp claws ever grown, and those claws had Rolly by the right wrist, just above his useless protective glove.

"Cak," the bird said.

"Ahhh . . ." Rolly said, when he spotted me out of the corner of his eye. He had one of the hawk's legs trapped in his left gloved hand along with part of the netting, and he wasn't letting go. "Help."

"Cora Mae," I said into the radio. "Where are you?"

I jumped when she said, "Right here," from behind me. She moved alongside me, one broken shoe in her hand. "What should we do?"

The Cooper's hawk continued to dig in while giving me a stare from its orange eyeball. Blood trickled down Rolly's arm.

"Let go, Rolly," I advised. "It's a standoff at the moment, but the bird's going to win because you're losing blood. Next time, wear longer gloves."

"Help," he continued to squawk.

The hawk said nothing, but now it had its

beak wrapped around Rolly's right arm and was trying to get a good hold.

"I'm not getting close," Cora Mae announced when I looked at her. "Gertie, hit it with something."

I wasn't sure if the "it" she referred to was the Cooper's hawk or Rolly, but I wasn't getting involved in the government's problems if I could help it. I certainly wasn't going to lose any of my own blood for him.

"Let go," I said to Rolly again. "He's going to sever an artery. I've got a hold on him. He won't get away."

Another lie. But Rolly had his eyes squeezed shut and wouldn't know that. Besides, by now I'd accepted the fact that a private investigator has to commit to a life of deception. In other words, the end justifies the means. Or is it the means justifies the end?

Just when I thought I'd have to kick Rolly in the shins, he let go of the hawk's leg.

Before I could blink, the bird was in the air, wings fluttering and soaring straight for the woodline.

The mice, sensing a unique opportunity to survive, beat it through the torn netting and scrambled for cover in the field. However, they found their path to freedom blocked by my good friend, the shoeless

Cora Mae. She screamed her head off and jumped around like she was walking across hot coals.

"Another reason to wear sturdy shoes," I said, watching a frightened mouse race over her bare toes.

She continued to alert every critter in the U.P. until she ran out of air. That woman really has a set of lungs.

"I'm hurt bad," Rolly moaned through the noise. "You'll have to apply a tourniquet. I'll be lucky to make it to the hospital before I bleed out."

I studied his wounds. "You're overreacting. All you need is a couple of butterfly band-aids. I have some in here someplace."

"What you doing out in the woods with a suitcase?" Rolly wanted to know while I dug through my weapons purse.

The remark didn't deserve a reply.

After bandaging him up, I said to Cora Mae, who forgot about her own problems once the mice disappeared and she noticed the blood, "Get your handcuffs out. I'm making a citizen's arrest."

I've always wanted to say that.

"Hold on there," Rolly said.

With fluid cunning, I reached into my purse and turned on my micro-recorder in case he was going to confess.

158

"I saw you from up in the tree stand," I said. "You're poaching birds. You should be ashamed of yourself, using your position to steal protected raptors."

"I'm not stealing anything." Rolly pressed on the bandages and winced. "I'm checking flight patterns and health and gathering data. Didn't you see the band around its leg?"

"I don't know what you're talking about," I said, but I'd seen the band.

"That's how we identify them, by the bands. Then we know where they came from. I was going to record information in this book here and inspect it for infectious diseases." Rolly held up a notebook. "And then I was going to let it go."

"Sounds reasonable to me," Cora Mae said, watching the ground for lingering mice. "You dragged me all the way out here for nothing."

It was possible that our inept game warden was telling the truth.

I dug the red tooth out of my pocket and held it out in my palm for Rolly to see. "What do you make of this?" I said.

"Bear tooth," he grunted. "Where'd you get that?"

"Over there," I waved vaguely at the woods. "Why's it red?"

"Here's what we do." Rolly puffed out his chest as if he was delivering a keynote speech at the Warden of the Year Dinner. "We put out piles of sardines with different dyes, depending on the area, and it works into their teeth. Bears can travel a long way, but usually they stay in the same ten or fifteen miles. Though I seen 'em swimming across Lake Superior. Those coming from Canada or from across the lake don't have any dye at all."

"What's the point of the dye?" I asked.

"If you shoot a bear you have to bring it to a DNR office. Besides using it for research and stuff, we can trace the dye to make sure it wasn't killed out of the area where the hunter applied for a license. Tricky, hey?"

"Well, where do you use the red dye?"

Rolly rubbed his chin, thinking hard. "Not around here. Tamarack County is blue. Maple County, that's it. Wait a minute." His eyes narrowed. "Let's take a little walk and check out this tree stand you say you were sitting in. And just for fun, let's take a look at your bear license. And I'm confiscating that tooth."

I turned off the recorder.

"You need to get to the hospital right away," I said. "Those band-aids won't hold for long and I don't have anymore."

"I'm feeling pretty good," he said. "Let's go."

We walked into the woods, and I tried to dissuade him, but his mind was made up. He was determined to arrest the woman who had just saved his life.

"I don't have a weapon," I said. "How could I be shooting illegally without one?"

"It's around here someplace," he insisted. "Let's start by searching this here motorsickle."

He walked around the bike looking for stash places, then thoroughly searched the area around the tree stand. He even crawled up into the tree and inspected the platform before reluctantly giving up and releasing us.

The only thing he forgot to check for was a motorsickle license.

Kitty was waiting for us by the side of the Trouble Buster when we roared up to Jackie's house and parked the bike.

Her mouth fell open. "I wish I had a camera," she said.

I peeled off the helmet and glanced at Kitty's rusty old Lincoln. "What's Fred doing here," I said, watching him try to eat his way through the window to get to me.

"Look how he's bonded to you, Gertie," Cora Mae said. "Isn't that cute? Someone better let him out before he destroys the inside of Kitty's car."

Kitty opened the door and he bounded out, nearly bowling me over.

"I went to your place to see what you were up to and Grandma Johnson made me take him. He's been lugubrious without you."

"And you're quite loquacious today," I replied.

"You two are going to drive me to drink," Cora Mae complained.

"I'll drive you anywhere you want to go, Honey," Kitty said. "But it's a little early in the day for hitting the bottle."

"We have work to do," I reminded them. "Did Grandma say whether or not she's heard any word on Little Donny?"

"Nothing yet."

After digging my maps out of the glove compartment, I flipped down the truck's tailgate, sorted through them, and spread out a map of Maple County. Fred, now that he'd found me, leaped up into the truck bed to make himself comfy. A stack of maps flew to the ground as he plunked down right in the center of the action, his red devil eyes locked onto me.

I rearranged everything, then unfolded the

falconer's list from the Marquette DNR office. "Kitty, help me find a falconer in Maple County. I'm tracking a red tooth and a bird feather. I don't know how they connect, but I'm going to follow them to the end."

She studied the list. "Um . . . um," said our fancy word specialist. "Um . . . Try this one on Crevice Road."

We bent over the map looking for Crevice Road. "Here it is. Are there any more on the list that might be in Maple County?"

"Um . . . um . . . um . . ." Kitty shook her head. "Nope. That's it."

I read the name of the falconer out loud, "Ted Latvala."

Cora Mae slipped her rump up on the open tailgate as I folded the map. "Why are we chasing birds and bears, Gertie? Shouldn't we be searching for Little Donny?"

I shook my head. "We tried that and came up with nothing. If we can't figure out the future, we have to go back to the past. The dead warden didn't show up at Carl's bait pile alone. We have to find out where he was and who he was with."

"And that'll lead us to Little Donny?" Cora Mae said.

I had a charley horse in my chest and I

163

couldn't look her in the eye when I answered, "That's right."

Maybe I couldn't bring Little Donny back, but I was determined to find out the truth, no matter what.

Truth is a slippery concept. It changes shape according to who's speaking it and it never looks the same to any two people. That's why it's so elusive. Or illusive, as I always say.

"Everybody ready?" I asked after gathering up the maps.

"Cora Mae and I should take one last shot at the woods," Kitty said. "We'll start at Carl's bait pile and head toward Walter's place. Maybe we missed something."

"I broke my shoe. I can't possibly go," Cora Mae said. "And I'm sick of the woods."

"I have a pair of boots in my trunk," Kitty said. "You can wear them."

"Watch your backs," I said while I tried to coax Fred out of the back of the truck.

"What do you mean by that?" Cora Mae wanted to know.

"Those arrows in Billy's back were meant for Little Donny."

"I was hoping you wouldn't put that together," Kitty said. "I already thought of it."

"Billy found Little Donny's cap. That's why he's dead right now instead of my grandson."

If Little Donny was still alive, he was in big trouble.

ELEVEN

Crevice Road lay about a mile in from the main road. They named it that for a good reason. Michigan's transportation department is in no hurry to repair our roads, so I weaved along, avoiding the worst of the potholes.

Gravel and dust kicked up behind me and I kept glancing in the back of the truck to make sure Fred was okay. He'd absolutely refused to abandon the back even after I pulled and pushed on him for a while.

Now he sat there, fat and sassy, like he rode in the back of trucks all the time, and maybe he did. He and I were in the early stages of getting to know each other, and so far he'd been full of surprises.

I pulled into Ted Latvala's driveway and parked behind enough rattletrap, rusted-out vehicles to fill a junkyard. I counted three outbuildings and guessed there might be more behind the tree line, where I saw the beginning of a wide, worn trail leading into the woods.

Grabbing a clipboard, I gruffly reminded Fred to stay put, walked to the front door of the house, and rapped loudly.

Smoke drifted lazily from a chimney and I could smell the aroma from a woodburning stove. One of my favorite smells is burning wood. I sucked in a big breathful of it as the door jerked open.

The man glaring at me had more hair than any man I'd ever seen. A dark curly mop sprung from his head, whiskers cascaded down his chin, and more of it sprouted from the front of his red plaid shirt and crept up his neck to meet the beard. Even the back of his hands were hairy.

"What?" he growled.

I cleared my throat. "Yes, well, I'm with the census bureau and I —"

"You have ten seconds to get off my property." He brandished a shotgun hanging loose from one of his hairy hands.

"And then?"

"And then I start shooting. I'll blow your head off."

In the space that read "Number of people living in dwelling," I marked "one." With all that hair and the nasty disposition, there couldn't be anyone else in the house.

"Just a minute," I said, because I could see he was getting antsy. "Have a little patience." I shoved the clipboard between my knees and dug through the weapons purse on my shoulder. Triumphantly I held up my new sheriff's badge.

"I'd like to ask you a few questions," I said.

He scowled at the badge. Then his eyes took in my Trouble Buster truck, where Fred was beading in on us with rapt attention.

"That's a fake badge," he said, sneering at me.

I turned the badge around and studied it. "How could you tell," I said.

"No cop would be caught dead driving in that truck. *Trouble Buster?* You crazy or what?"

I hadn't used my stun gun yet today and was considering zapping him when I heard him cock the shotgun. There's no sound like it in the world, and if you're on the receiving end, nothing is scarier.

Fred and I hightailed it down the gravel road.

The Deer Horn Restaurant was hopping as I drove through Stonely, and it reminded me of how hungry I was. The train stopped on the tracks across the street from the restaurant meant that Otis Knutson was inside.

I could drive on home and make a sandwich for lunch, but then I'd have to face Grandma Johnson's snaky tongue and Heather's hound-dog eyes.

The two of them were going to give me an ulcer sooner or later. Besides, I enjoyed talking to Otis, so I swung in.

"What you got in the back of your truck?" Carl called from a table he shared with Otis. "A bear?"

"If that's a bear," Otis said, "it's still alive. I just saw it move."

"Hey Ruthie, you got any roadkill on the menu?" Carl called out, tipping back on his chair.

"What kind of vegetable goes with road-kill?" Otis asked.

"Squash," Carl replied.

I'd gone through this routine already only about a hundred times. It's easy to entertain Yoopers, and a good joke stays around for a long time.

"You're not going to sit with these two old fools," Ruthie exclaimed as she set plates in front of Carl and Otis.

"I need a laugh today, Ruthie."

"I hear ya. What'll it be?"

"Coffee and a grilled cheese sandwich," I said, eyeing the mounds of meat and potatoes and carrots steaming on the men's plates.

All the while we ate our lunch, Fred sang a song of sorrow from the back of the truck. He'd let out a mournful yowl, then swing his eyes over at the restaurant window. I gave him a few waves to let him know I hadn't forgotten him.

"Dog looks rabid," Carl observed, shifting his eyes to the right, then to the left, then over my head. "Where'd you get him?"

"He's a retired police dog, search and rescue."

More like search and destroy, but that was a secret.

When Ruthie poured another round of coffee I saw Blaze's sheriff truck pull in and park right next to the Trouble Buster.

I thought about hiding in the ladies' room but I couldn't leave Fred to fend for himself, not to mention that the restaurant was the size of a hunting shack and my son would find me eventually. I shouldn't have worried about Fred because Blaze stopped and rubbed his big, black head. Fred could have conducted an orchestra with his tail.

Blaze stood back from my truck and peered at the lettering meandering along the side. He scowled at me through the window.

"Carl," I said, "you're going to have to help me out here. Tell Blaze you have been driving me around."

"You want me to lie to a law enforcement official?"

"It's only Blaze."

"But Gertie, he'll know it's a lie. My station wagon is out there."

By now, Blaze had ripped open the restaurant door and was stalking my way. He nodded at the two men and leaned over me, throwing his sheriff's hat down on the table like a gauntlet.

I'm used to his intimidating ways. It takes more than this overgrown kid to rattle my cage.

I grinned. "Sit down," I said. "I'll buy you lunch."

"Outside. Right now."

Rather than create a scene in Ruthie's restaurant, I waited for him to pick up his hat and I followed him out. Behind Otis' train a stand of jack pines reached for the sky. I saw a hawk riding the air currents, scouting for a meal.

Blaze puffed himself up and his face grew flushed, like he was short of breath. Before he could say anything, Carl rushed out of the restaurant with a carry-out bag in his arms.

"Wait, Blaze," he called out. "I can explain."

While Carl bamboozled Blaze, I crept over to the back of the truck, rubbed Fred's ears, and reviewed the case.

The feather hadn't amounted to much. I wasn't any closer to learning the source of the one found on the bottom of the dead warden's shoe than the day I discovered it.

It had been a long shot anyway.

"I'm having a hard time believing what you're telling me, Carl," Blaze said from the other side of the truck. "Your car is right here. How do you explain that?"

"I left it for Otis. He wants to go see his . . . ah . . . his . . . ah, mother."

"Otis can't leave his train on the tracks while he goes visiting. It's one thing to stop for a bite to eat, but that isn't exactly a parking space."

"Well, I'll go tell him that, then."

I heard the restaurant door bang shut as Carl hurried back in. Blaze stomped over.

"This is getting embarrassing," he said. "I could handle the money buried in a box and you spray-painting my truck with yellow paint." He stopped to glare at his old truck, now mine. "And I didn't say a word when you took up with Cora Mae, but . . ."

I stared him in the eye.

"But this truck," he continued. "And the lettering and you running around without a driver's license, thinking you're Lieutenant Columbo. You've gone too far."

"You should be out looking for Little Donny," I said, louder than I intended. Part of my tactic with Blaze was to never show anger. "You're more concerned about catching me driving than you are about finding your nephew."

I poked him in the chest. "Maybe I shouldn't have to do your job."

Blaze hitched up his pants.

I turned to the road with my arms crossed.

Carl came back out and Blaze walked over to talk to him again.

I watched a white van moving steadily toward me along M35 and wandered over to the side of the restaurant to get away from all the noisy chatter.

The van pulled to a stop at the only four-way flashing traffic light in town. I saw the name on the side of the vehicle. Mitch Movers.

Right then, I decided to abandon the feather theory and the search for falconers and the bear with the missing red tooth. I vowed to resume my search for Little

Donny. Dead or alive, I'd find my grandson.

The truck edged forward and started to gather speed as it passed me.

Then it happened.

A bird feather exactly like the one on the bottom of Warden Hendricks' shoe fluttered in the wind created by the moving van and landed at my feet. I stared at the back of the van. Another feather spit into the air.

I broke into a run.

"Carl," I shouted. "It's time to go. Hurry."

But by the time I got Carl untangled from Blaze's law-and-order speech and into the driver's seat of my truck, it was way too late to catch up with the van.

"This sure smells good," I said, opening Carl's leftover bag and peeking inside. He had enough food inside to feed a black bear for a week.

"Stay out of my bag," Carl said, hands on the steering wheel at ten and two o'clock. "And Blaze is still behind us."

I sighed and turned to check. "Take me home. That's all we can do."

Blaze continued on past us when we turned into my driveway. "Stay a while," I said to Carl. "I'll take you back when I'm sure he's really gone."

"I'll go in and visit with Grandma Johnson," he said.

"You always were a brave one. I'll put your bag in the fridge."

I found Cora Mae and Kitty leaning against my fence watching George work. His rattlesnake cowboy hat was tipped onto one of the pickets and he'd stripped down to his jeans and boots. George at sixty still had the physique of a young construction worker.

"Thought I'd work on building your sauna," George said. "The ladies are helping."

I could see that.

Cora Mae was draped over the fence as close to George as possible without actually impeding his movements. She looked like a lean she-cat, with her black heels and tight black pants and confident expression on her face. It was only a matter of time before she mauled George and hauled him into her den.

"I thought you two were going to search for Little Donny," I said to Kitty and Cora Mae. "From what I can tell, based on my experienced investigator skills, he isn't out this way."

"Some of us," Kitty said, tipping her head at Cora Mae, "got a little distracted."

The guinea hens must have been in the

outer field when we pulled in because I saw them heading our way, running in a pack. They veered off before reaching us, and I heard a yip from the other side of the barn, along with a lot of hen chatter.

I called Fred, and he came bounding for cover with the hens right behind him. He ran in close to me and I flapped my arms like wings to keep the hens at bay.

George grinned. "Those hens sure hate Fred."

"They just sense that he's afraid of them," I explained. "Once he stands up for himself, they'll back off."

"What's new with you?" George asked, coming and standing right next to me. I admired the few boards rising from a foundation that would support my new sauna.

"Someone around here is smuggling birds illegally," I announced. "They're using moving vans to transport them."

Kitty snapped her fingers. "Mitch Movers, I'll bet. I've seen that white van more than once and wondered where it came from."

I nodded. "Feathers blew out of the van when it passed the Deer Horn. I was standing right by the road when it happened but I couldn't follow it because Blaze would have arrested me."

176

"Why would he have arrested you?" George wanted to know.

"I don't have a clue," I lied.

"Gertie doesn't have a driver's license," Cora Mae squealed and George started laughing.

"That's easy enough to correct," he said through his guffaws.

"You haven't driven with her, have you?" Race Car Kitty said. "It won't be that easy. And she failed her written test."

"Well, let me know if you want some pointers," George offered, giving my arm a little squeeze. A jolt of electricity shot down to my toes and my knees threatened to buckle.

I leaned against the fence. "Let me tell you more about the bird thieves," I said weakly.

"What kind of birds," George asked.

"Red-tailed hawks, peregrines, you name it." I like to add interest to my stories. I might not have all the licenses the government imposes on its citizens but I do have a literary license. "Bald eagles for all I know."

"But what are they doing with them?" Cora Mae asked.

"You can't buy raptors in a store," I explained. "The only way to get one is to capture it in the wild, find a sponsor, and go through a lot of governmental red tape. My guess is, they're stealing birds and eggs and selling them for a profit."

"People want them for pets?" Kitty asked.

"No, they train them for hunting. Rabbits, squirrels." I looked over at my guard hens that were pecking through the gravel in the drive. "Guineas."

"We stumbled right into the middle of a crime ring," Kitty shouted in excitement, throwing her beefy arm up in the air in a triumphant gesture.

"We sure did." I edged closer to George. "Dealing in illegal birds is a dangerous and profitable business, and that's why they're hunting Little Donny. He knows who they are. It could even be the Russian mafia."

"Do you think the dead warden was part of it?" Kitty asked. "That would certainly obfuscate the issue."

"Kitty," I said, realizing I needed to expand my word list pronto if I expected to keep up. "Did you go to college?"

"Sure did."

"Did you graduate?"

"Yup."

"You need to go to law school and put those fancy words to real use."

Law classes would keep her busy while I boned up on my vocabulary.

Kitty's grin spread like butter on hot toast. "I'll look into it. Maybe I can register for one of those on-line classes. But that will be after this case. I'm your bodyguard, remember, and I take my job seriously."

George picked his cowboy hat from the picket fence and adjusted it on his head. "I better get back to work."

"We better get back to work, too," I said.

"I'll stay here and be the look-out for Little Donny," Cora Mae said, attaching to the fence again.

"I have a special project for you," I told her. "You have to come along."

No way was I leaving her with George.

Twelve

My daughter Star's twin boys, Ed and Red, own Herb's Bar, which is the only watering hole in Stonely. Since there isn't much to do in this town other than eat and drink, business starts early in the day at Herb's.

No one knows exactly why the bar is called Herb's, because the chain of ownership doesn't include anyone named Herb. That's been the biggest mystery in Stonely until recently when Little Donny went missing and a dead warden was pulled off Carl's bait pile. Then the Herb puzzle took a back seat.

As soon as Kitty pulled open the door of the bar, conversation inside died and everyone who had bellied up to the bar swung around to watch us enter.

It's a harrowing experience for a newcomer, but I was used to the ways of the clannish Swedes and Finns.

A few people mumbled greetings when

they recognized us. Then the customers went back to whatever business had been interrupted by our entrance. If they hadn't known us, though, the place would have stayed dead quiet for a lot longer.

"I can't stand all the smoke," Cora Mae crabbed as soon as she had the chance, still miffed that I had hauled her from the construction site. "And it's four o'clock in the afternoon." She scrunched her nose. "Look at the clientele."

Cora Mae was starting to sound like Grandma Johnson, but she did have a point about the afternoon crowd. Most of them looked like their wells went dry at the beginning of August and they hadn't bathed since.

"A private investigator has to be flexible," I said. Kitty slid her solid frame onto a bar stool. She had removed her pin curls for the evening, but, as usual, she hadn't combed out her hair, causing a spring-loaded reaction with her curls. Her enormous thighs spilled over the seat and her knees were dangerously far apart.

Someone across the bar winked at her and she fluttered a wave. I did a double take, thinking I might be hallucinating.

The twins were working the back of the bar as if they were connected at the hip, sidling around each other in fluid motion while they served customers.

"Hi, Granny," Ed called out, sliding a beer down to me. "What would your friends like?"

The three of us sat in a line at the bar with tall beers in front of us and a hunk of on-the-house beef jerky in our hands.

"Holy cripes," Cora Mae said, still in complaint mode. "This jerky is going to rip my teeth out."

"I'll take yours," Kitty said, reaching over.

Cora Mae gave her a mean look and cradled her jerky next to her body. This raging hormonal thing always happens when she doesn't have a steady boyfriend.

"What happened to BB and the other Detroit boys?" I asked, hoping to steer her thoughts away from George.

"They'll be around later tonight," she said, perking up a little. "Want to go with us?"

"I'm behind on my work," I lied, wondering how long I'd be employed if I didn't wrap this case up quickly. "Did you find anything in the woods today?"

Cora Mae leaned on the bar with one elbow and one Wonderbra'd boob spilled over her arm. Every man along the bar leaned forward, too. "We didn't get far. It's a long way from Carl's bait pile to Walter's house. Kitty got tired."

"Me!" Kitty exclaimed. "I thought you were the one complaining all along the trail."

"I was up for it."

"You were not."

By this brief glimpse into my partners' afternoon hours, I was able to deduce that nothing at all had been accomplished.

"Tell us your theory," Kitty said, sipping her beer and coming up with a foam mustache. "What do you think happened?"

"I'm convinced that someone is stealing or raising birds and selling them, and Warden Hendricks must have found out."

"Do you think a local is in on it?" Kitty asked.

"What about Rolly?" Cora Mae suggested.

"Rolly Akkala couldn't handle a cooked goose," I said, remembering his fight with the Cooper's hawk. "Walter Laakso is a possibility. His place is next to the spot where the ATV was discovered, but I didn't see any signs of trapped birds when we were there the other day."

"Marlin, Remy, and BB are from Detroit," Kitty said. "You know how it is in that city. They might be up to more than hunting bears."

"We'll keep an eye on them," Cora Mae said, sweeping her head around the room looking for fresh meat.

The door opened, the noise in the room stopped abruptly, and the customers at the bar eyed Onni Maki coming in. Then everything started up again.

Onni Maki was shriveled up like a dried-out puffball mushroom and considered himself the most eligible bachelor in Stonely. There aren't a lot of available men living in the north woods, but I'd rather kiss a porcupine than consider letting that old coot get near me.

"Hi, ladies," he said, with his typical leer, dripping gold chains and cheap cologne.

"Not now, Onni," I said. "Ed, I'm buying Onni a beer. Set it down over there." I pointed to the far end of the bar.

Helmi Salo called out to him and he redirected, slinking away.

"That white truck was coming down M35 from the north," I said.

"Marquette?" Kitty said.

I nodded. "Or just this side of Marquette. Maple County."

"What's next?" Cora Mae said, leaning in. "Do we have a plan?"

"We're going to spread out," I replied, lowering my voice. "Start up conversations and see if anyone in here knows anything about suspicious moving vans or illegal birds."

The three of us spent the next two hours interrogating everyone in the bar. Aside from a few pointers on the best bear bait and several bear facts that I didn't need to know, nothing much came of it.

"I'm tellin' ya they can swim right across Lake Superior," someone said. "Or Lake Michigan for that matter."

"Naw, no way. How many beers you had?" someone else said.

"How much you want to bet? I'm tellin' ya the Coast Guard picked up a black bear eight miles out and he was swimmin' the other way."

"Naw, no way."

Multitasker that I am, I had my clipboard and a list of names, and I knocked off three more census stops right there at the bar while keeping my ears open for worthwhile news.

Cora Mae came up empty-handed and Kitty locked in a date for next Saturday night.

Johnson family dinners are like shootouts at the OK Corral. Grandma Johnson pumps her semi-automatic venom through her new snapping teeth, Blaze tries to hog-tie me to the kitchen sink since he's in competition with me and seems to be losing, and Heather and my baby, Star, run blockade.

But first we eat.

Heather had put out quite a spread, whipping up a meal from my family recipe box — creamed rutabaga, mashed potatoes with creamed corn scooped on the top, and pan-fried chicken.

I should include the creamed rutabaga in my future cookbook. I thought it tasted better when someone else made it.

"Where's Mary?" Star asked Blaze. "I haven't seen her for a few days."

"She's still feeling poorly."

I was sure she was making up excuses in case Grandma Johnson decided to cook another one of her roasted chickens.

Blaze looked a bit haggard from putting in so many hours.

After the meal, I cut everyone a thick square of apple crisp, made with juicy apples right from my own tree. Blaze poured heavy cream over his and pushed his expanding belly back from the table to make more room.

Star, wearing a cute, fuzzy pink sweater, started what I call the family hum, and we all joined in. "Hummmmmm . . ." we all intoned.

Grandma Johnson, as usual, ruined the mood and I wondered for the umpteenth time how she managed to move into my house right under my nose without more of a fight from me.

Blaze keeps talking about selling her house, but that's where I draw the line. If she isn't going into a nursing home, she's going back to her own house someday. I'm viewing this as a temporary situation.

"Why don't you ever make my Spam casserole?" Grandma Johnson said, winding up to fire a few rounds now that dessert was on the table.

"I'll make it tomorrow," Heather said quickly, when she saw me open my mouth to reply. "Or that meatloaf you make that won the prize at the fair."

"That's good, too," Grandma admitted, and I could have jumped up and kissed Heather for redirecting Grandma.

I'd rather eat her raw chicken than the Spam casserole any day.

"Someone thinks they spotted Little Donny in Newberry," Blaze announced. "Deputy Snell and Deputy Sheedlo are checking it out."

Heather clapped her hands together and I saw a hint of the first smile since she arrived in Stonely. "That's wonderful news."

"Probably running away on foot," Grandma Johnson clacked. "To get as far away as he can. That rascal never should have shot the sheriff."

"That was a warden, Grandma," Star said. "And he didn't shoot him."

"Gertie put him up to it," she insisted. "Or *that woman*."

"Cora Mae has nothing to do with this," I said. "Blaze, why would he be in Newberry? That's a lot of miles east of here. Nothing's up there."

Blaze shrugged. "We have to follow every lead."

"Who's your source?"

"Don't know. Someone called the sighting in and hung up."

"I wish you'd take care of it yourself instead of sending Dickey."

It would be great to get rid of Blaze for a while. If Little Donny was in Newberry, which I doubted, cat-hair-crusted Dickey and his no-neck cohort could trip right over him and never know it was him. Especially since they retired the only one in the trio with any brains.

"I asked you to quit calling him Dickey, Ma. That's disrespectful."

"You better stay in town and watch this

188

place," Grandma advised him. "The British will be here any day and we'll need all the reinforcement we can get. I'll cover the front of the house and you take the back. Anyone know where my weapon is?"

Too bad Mary wasn't here to witness more of Grandma's slippage, since she's Grandma's most ardent defender.

Just for the record, I taped the conversation with my new micro-recorder.

Kitty blew through Stonely's one and only four-way stop sign like she was Otis' train with a broken brake system.

"You're supposed to obey those signs even after dark," I said, pretty sure of my facts. I'd been studying the driver's-testing booklet. I didn't remember any mention of the proper procedure after dark, but common sense would tell you that the same rules applied as during the day.

Unless, of course, nobody was around to see it. Which in this case, there definitely was.

"You almost sideswiped Onni Maki," I said, a little louder, noting the surprised look on his wrinkled face when we careened past him with only an inch or two to spare.

Kitty had that crazed look she always gets when she's behind the wheel, and I thought, briefly, of belting up. Ordinarily Yoopers don't wear seat belts because most of us aren't in any hurry and we're driving nice and slow. Besides, seat belts make us feel confined. But Kitty had me reconsidering.

I glanced back to see how Fred was handling this from the Lincoln's back seat. He had his head turned, and while I watched, he opened his mouth wide and yawned, slow and relaxed. That dog is made of reinforced iron.

"You think they'll be on the road this late?" Kitty said. "I don't see any vestigial evidence that the truck is still around."

I sighed. It was my turn and I didn't feel like playing anymore. "Time out," I said, making a football 'T' sign with my hands. "You win this round." I didn't have any idea what vestigial meant, but in a few days I'd come back stronger than ever.

Kitty nodded an acknowledgment but didn't rub her win in my face. "How far north should we drive?"

"I don't know," I said. "The moving van I saw by the restaurant could have come from any place to the north. We'll need a little dumb luck to find it."

"We've seen it several times in the last few days, so I think our odds are pretty good."

I glanced at the speedometer. It said

eighty-five, but we were on a straightaway so I kept calm and devised a plan to save all of our lives.

A private detective lives by her wits.

"I have a better idea," I said, slyly. "Why don't we turn down a side road and wait there. Then we'll catch them coming or going."

"Brilliant," Kitty said, slamming on the brakes until the car was practically doing a handstand. I reached out for the dashboard with locked elbows and could hear Fred scrambling for solid footing.

Kitty whipped the car to the right and did a Uu-turn on two wheels, with gravel flying everywhere. She stopped on the edge of a narrow side road where we had a good view of Highway M35.

I hunted around on the floor to find my weapons purse and its scattered contents. It took all my willpower not to zap Kitty with the stun gun, which had rolled under the seat during her stunt driving.

Two hours later we were still sitting tight. Kitty had fallen asleep, her head against the headrest, her mouth wide open, and the oddest collection of snorts and gulps emanating from her cavernous mouth. I didn't mind because the noise kept me alert. Fred dozed in the back, occasionally rising to peer out into the blackest night I'd ever seen. Not a single star beamed down on us, and the moon didn't offer even a slice of light.

I wished I'd remembered to bring snacks along. Usually on a surveillance run we have an entire picnic basket — fried chicken and all the trimmings. Tonight's run was impromptu and therefore without all the fringe benefits associated with a planned event.

I gave Kitty a little nudge and her eyes flew open.

"Let's call it a night," I said once her face lost that cloudy, confused expression.

Kitty reached forward to start the car just as a white moving van shot by, heading north toward Marquette and Maple County. She jerked her head in my direction.

"I saw it," I screeched, excited to have a plan that was finally panning out. Most of our stakeouts are exercises in futility, but this one was going to pay off.

We ripped out onto the two-lane M35 and turned toward the taillights fading in the distance. I didn't have to suggest to my partner that we were in need of speed. Kitty accelerated and the G-forces snapped my head against the headrest.

About a half mile down the road we caught up. Kitty pulled out into the other lane and came alongside the van. The driver did a double take and I slammed my new sheriff's badge against the window and motioned him over.

He held up one particularly offensive finger and continued driving.

Kitty laid on the horn.

The driver reached onto the dashboard and flipped open a cell phone.

"He's calling for reinforcements," I shouted. "We need to stop him right now before his backup shows up."

An oncoming car forced Kitty to take evasive action. She let up on the gas, pulled in behind the van until the approaching car passed, then roared alongside again.

This time she gave his front bumper a little tap with her own rusted-out front bumper. That's the beauty of driving a junker. You can let your creativity flow without expensive consequences.

After the second love tap, the driver slowed the van and pulled over. Kitty's Lincoln hugged his bumper all the way.

"Are you nuts, lady?" he shouted, jumping out of the van and wrenching my door open.

Fred growled menacingly, showing a collection of large sharp fangs. While the driver was wondering what to do about the devil dog in the back seat, I took the opportunity to hit him in the chest with my super-charged stun gun. He went down hard and fast, like a boulder flung from Lake Superior's high shoreline. Once down in the dirt, he started twitching.

While he rolled around on the ground trying to figure out what hit him, Kitty and I ran to the back of the van and pulled the doors open.

"We need a flashlight," I said, running back to the car and digging through my weapons purse until I found it.

Kitty had already crawled into the back of the van when she reached out for the flashlight. I handed it to her and crawled in next to her.

We watched the light move from one end of the van to the other. I grabbed it from her and repeated the process.

We looked at each other, speechless.

The inside of the van was as clean as one of Grandma Johnson's plucked chickens. Not a single bird or egg or feather of any kind.

The driver moaned and I noticed that he had staggered to his feet. Fred, joining in the fray, lunged through my open door and forced the man back against the truck.

"Good boy, Fred," I said, proud of my

team in spite of my disappointment over the missing evidence.

Then I heard the siren in the distance. "I thought you called your partners in crime," I said urgently to the driver. "Who did you really call?"

"Nith oneth oneth," he said, spittle running down his chin.

"Cops," Kitty called to me, jumping from the van. "He called the cops."

Since we weren't sure which side of the law we were on at the moment, and considering that some people thought a stun gun was an illegal weapon, Kitty and I took one last peek in the front of the van, shooed Fred into the car, and hit the road.

The Lincoln fish-tailed onto the old highway, did a U-turn, and a few seconds later we passed a vehicle speeding toward the moving van, running lights and siren.

"Dang," I said. "That was Blaze."

"Good thing I turned the headlights off," Kitty said. "I don't think he saw us."

Earlier, I had wanted stars and the glow of the moon, but at least a few things were going my way tonight, so we slunk home under cover of darkness.

Before going to bed, I put my stun gun on the charger.

THIRTEEN

"I know that was you and Kitty out there last night!" Blaze shouted in my face. He sat at my kitchen table drinking my coffee and sucking down my sugar doughnuts, and I couldn't believe the way he was treating me once his mouth was empty. "Little bitty red-haired old lady, the driver said. And a Loch Ness monster. You and that fat friend of yours fit the description perfectly."

Blaze then pointed at Fred, lying by the door. "And he fits the guy's description of a vicious, wild wolf that came close to shredding him into pieces."

"Shush," I said, slightly offended by the "old lady" description. "Or you'll wake up Grandma and Heather. They need their rest." I took a long sip of coffee before replying. "My truck was here at the house all night. You can ask anyone in the family once they get up. And that 'vicious wolf' is the result of your police training."

Blaze didn't hear me, which isn't unusual.

He held up his cigar-fat fingers and ticked off his complaints. "Impersonating an officer by identifying yourself as a law enforcement official," he said. "Using a dog as a deadly weapon, attempting to hijack a vehicle." He looked up. "I don't know what you did to the driver but he was a mess, so let's include aggravated assault of some kind in the charges."

When Blaze put it like that, it *did* sound pretty bad.

"I wouldn't be surprised to find out you had a gun in your purse."

"Go ahead," I said, throwing my almost-empty weapons purse across the table. "Search your own mother's personal belongings like she's some kind of common criminal. Instead of locating your nephew, you're busy harassing your mother."

I had anticipated this moment and had stashed the questionable items away in my underwear drawer. "If you want to arrest all your family members, you should know that Grandma Johnson had a pistol when she moved in here. I took it away from her and hid it the first time she waved it in my face and threatened to shoot me. Maybe you can handcuff her and rough her up a little."

Blaze ignored me.

After sorting through the purse and finding nothing, he glared at me and said, "You're lucky the driver you assaulted isn't pressing charges."

I snorted. Of course he wouldn't press charges. He was engaged in criminal activity and didn't want to call too much attention to himself. I was surprised he called nine-one-one in the first place.

A clean moving van didn't mean a clean life. I'd get him yet. Blaze might think the driver smelled like a rose, but I know skunk when it drives by.

"What was he doing out so late?" I asked. "Did you ask him that?"

"It's not any of my business or your business. There's no law says he can't drive his truck anytime and anywhere he wants to."

I snorted again.

"The only thing I haven't figured out," Blaze said, "is how you and Kitty got away. I didn't pass a single vehicle heading for Stonely, and the state trooper meeting me from Maple County said he didn't pass anyone either." He waved a finger in my face, which I hate. "I'm warning you . . ." he said, and let the sentence die away.

One of the best things the Finns and Swedes who settled in the U.P. brought over from

198

the old country was the sauna. We build them as separate little houses in our backyards, where we meet for social gatherings to share town gossip while throwing water on hot stones and sweating profusely.

Naked is the preferred mode of dress and in winter, after we're done perspiring, we roll around in the snow to finish off the process. That's why the sauna's location is so important. It needs to be well hidden from the road and the driveway.

We used to have a sauna behind the house until Blaze burned it down when he was about fourteen years old.

Never give a teenager a box of matches and instruct him to burn a pile of yard rubbish. Somehow the dry grass leading to the sauna caught fire and that was the end of our meeting place. By the time the local volunteers heard the fire siren going off in town and turned up, the damage was done. No one would've been able to guess that a sauna had ever existed on that patch of land.

George had made an offer to build a new one for me, and I found him working on it after Blaze blustered away.

It was a gorgeous September day. We'd had a frost overnight, and earlier this morning the lawn had been covered with a sparkly dusting of ice crystals. When the sun rose, it thawed things out.

"You're early this morning," I said, handing him a hot cup of coffee and sliding a napkin topped with a sugar doughnut onto the fence post. He picked it up and took a bite.

"You make the best doughnuts in Tamarack County, Gertie. Better include the recipe in your cookbook."

"Good idea," I said absently, more important things than doughnuts on my mind. "There's been no word from Little Donny, yet. It's been too long."

George gave me a gaze and I noticed that he'd cut himself shaving this morning. To me, that made him even more handsome and manly. "He'll turn up," he said. "Don't worry."

"I'm worried sick," I admitted, because George is my best male friend and I can count on him to understand. I watched while he took another bite of the doughnut. "If he's alive, where is he? He didn't have two nickels to rub together when he went into the woods. How would he feed himself? What would he eat? He doesn't know anything about survival in the wilderness."

George polished off the doughnut and took a long sip of coffee. "I wish I could reassure you. I know waiting is hard but that's all we can do right now."

Something was tugging at my memory — had been for awhile. Watching George eat that little piece of bakery started the gears in motion again.

"I'll see you later," I said, quickly heading for the house to gather my weapons, throw them in my purse, and grab my keys. "I have an idea."

I rushed to the truck, turned it around so the front end was facing the road, and leapt into the driver's seat to wait.

If what I thought was true, I'd find Little Donny this fine, crisp autumn morning.

"Where is Gertie?" I heard Grandma Johnson yell at George a little later. "She left the kitchen a big mess, flour and sugar from ceiling to floor. What kinda house am I having to live in?"

"Haven't seen her for a while," George yelled back.

"Well if she shows up, send her fanny right in here to clean this mess up. I'm having to do all the work around here."

Out of the rearview mirror, I watched Fred's big head come into view behind Grandma. She shrieked, opened the door wider, and whacked Fred's backside with a fly swatter to force him out of the house.

I almost gave up my hiding place to

defend Fred, but he didn't even notice the weak little tap coming from Grandma's scrawny arm. He strolled out the door and sniffed the air to catch a scent. She tried to give him another whack, but he turned his head to stare at her. She must have decided not to push her luck because she lowered the fly swatter, shrieked again, and slammed the door.

Fred headed for the truck and began to circle it at a trot.

Once I was sure that Grandma was safely back in the house, I opened the passenger door, Fred leapt into the cab, and we watched the world go by in slow motion.

A little later, Cora Mae and Kitty pulled up, but I ducked down in my seat, feeling the need for my own private space. Fred, sleeping by my side, was also out of view. From my side mirror I saw George come around from the back. Cora Mae fluffed her hair, bumped out her Wonderbra'd breasts, and went for him like a guided missile.

Kitty stomped over, too, and the three of them wandered toward the backyard.

I risked another peek out at the road. I worried that if I looked away from the road for even a second, that might be the exact time my target would drive by and I'd end up sitting here for nothing.

Sure enough, there he came, driving by without as much as a glance at my house, like a man on a mission.

I started the truck, intent on making a stealthy getaway. But Fred must have jiggled a few buttons when he jumped in, because the truck's siren started blaring. Kitty lumbered toward the driveway to see what the commotion was about, but I quickly turned off the siren and blew out of the yard.

So much for stealth.

But I had my man in my sights, and he didn't seem to react to the noise coming from my house.

Carl Anderson, the shifty-eyed sneak, sure seemed to be chowing down a lot of food lately. In fact, every time I saw him, he had extra food tucked in a bag under his arm. And that casserole.

What kind of Yooper male makes a casserole for his card-playing buddies? He'd be laughed right out of the game. Card-playing men brought jerky and beer and maybe a bag of chips to the table. That was it. And George knew nothing about any poker game that night.

And when was the last time Carl had asked about Little Donny?

Never. That's when. He'd never asked if Little Donny had been found.

Why?

Because he knew exactly where Little Donny was holed up. And Carl was feeding him.

Carl's station wagon turned right at the four-way stop in downtown Stonely, then made another right onto Porcupine Trail. I stayed back as far as I dared. The Trouble Buster stood out like a canary among sparrows, with its yellow paint job and fancy lettering, and I worried that he'd spot me.

It dawned on me that he was driving toward Porcupine Trail, and I thumped myself on the head with my hand for my denseness.

It should have been obvious all along.

Sure enough, I saw Carl pull into Grandma Johnson's driveway and hide his car from the road by driving around behind a row of cedars.

What a perfect hideout. Since Grandma was now living with me, her house was vacant and secluded, the ideal place to hide if people are searching for you.

I continued driving down Porcupine Trail until Carl had enough time to get inside the house. Then I swung around, ran the truck through a shallow ditch, and parked at the far end of my mother-in-law's property.

Fred and I trudged through the brush and approached the house from the rear. Peeking through a window, I saw Little Donny talking to Carl. I almost fell to my knees with relief. Instead, I wiped a stray tear away and sunk down under the window with my knees up by my chest while Fred mauled me and licked my face.

All I wanted to do was cry long and hard now that I knew my grandson was alive. Cry and hug him and then swat him and Carl for worrying me so much. But I knew I had to pull myself together.

"Get off me, you big slobber," I whispered to Fred, crawling from under the window and rising. "My grandson has some explaining to do. Let's go."

I wondered if having conversations with your dog was less crazy than babbling to yourself when no one else was around.

I guess it depended on whether or not the dog answered.

Fred grinned and ran for the steps.

"I must have been sleeping pretty soundly," Little Donny said, while we huddled at Grandma's kitchen table and watched him pound down Carl's bag of day-old bear bakery. He slapped his hands together to shake off the crumbs and didn't look like he'd been through nearly the wear-and-tear that I had trying to find him. "Because they were already by the bait pile when I woke up. I never heard them coming."

Carl chimed in. "There were two of them and they couldn't see Little Donny because he was stashed inside the brush in case a bear showed up." I had already guessed as much because I'd seen the flattened grass. "You were supposed to be awake and watching for bear action," Carl admonished him.

"Did they say anything?" I asked.

Little Donny nodded. "One said his integrity wasn't for sale and he wasn't going through with it. The other one didn't say anything, but the first one kept talking like he was trying to explain himself. Like he didn't want to have to do it but he had no choice. I couldn't see much because I was flat on the ground and the brush was thick. But I could see them from about the knees down. One had on brown pants like a uniform and the other wore green coveralls, the kind you buy at the farm and equipment store and he had on workboots."

"Then what happened?" I took my notebook out of my big purse and started writing.

"They began pushing each other, and I

couldn't believe it but the one with green coveralls ran over and grabbed my rifle that was leaning against the tree. The other guy started backing up, saying this could be worked out."

Little Donny's hand shook when he picked up his coffee cup and took a drink. "The overalled one said, 'Too late,' and he fired the rifle point-blank at the other guy, who fell over, and I knew right then he was dead. I almost died myself from shock."

I reached over and put a hand on his shoulder. "You've been through a lot for a nineteen-year-old."

Little Donny shoved another doughnut in his mouth to keep from bawling, and Carl helped out with the story. "Little Donny yelped when the rifle went off and the guy heard him. Isn't that right?"

Little Donny's eyes looked older than mine. "I took off running when he swung around. He pulled off another shot and I ran as hard as I could. He had an ATV that I didn't know about until I heard it start up, and then he was trying to chase me through the trees on the machine."

"Only Little Donny was smart," Carl added. "He kept moving through the denser woods where the ATV couldn't run. You raised 'em right, Gertie."

"Thanks, Carl," I said, chilled at how close I'd come to losing my grandson.

"While I ran, I dropped my clothes because orange is so easy to spot," Little Donny continued. "I'd stripped down to nothing but my pants, and then I found the thickest brush and hunkered down. He drove by without seeing me, but for a split second I thought I was a goner. Afterwards, I made my way here and jimmied the back door lock."

"Then he called me," Carl said. "Lucky for him, the phone wasn't disconnected."

I hadn't turned off any of Grandma Johnson's utilities because I hoped she'd move back home soon. My mental health depended on believing that.

"Your prints are on the arrows in Billy Lundberg's back," I said.

"I looked over Carl's arrows, thinking I might try bow hunting next time."

"Did you get a good look at the killer?"

"Not a real good look, but I think I'd know him if I saw him again."

"I asked the same thing," Carl said. "Little Donny said he didn't have any distinguishing features."

"A big guy," Little Donny said.

"All us Swedes and Finns are large," Carl replied. "It could have been anybody."

"Did he see you real good?" I needed to know.

Little Donny shrugged. "Probably about the same as I saw him."

"What happened to your cap?"

"Like I said, I flung everything off."

"And Billy found it and put it on."

To me, a flock of illegal birds hardly seemed like a motive for multiple murders.

"When Carl told me that a warrant had been issued for my arrest, we decided I better hide until this blows over."

Well, this situation wasn't a light breeze. It was more like a tornado, and I wasn't sure it would blow over without some interference on my part.

"You can't tell anyone that I'm here," Little Donny said.

"Your parents are suffering," I said.

"You know how mom is. Tell her and she'll never keep it a secret."

Heather was a blabbermouth. Always had been. "I'll see what I can do," I said.

"You can't hide forever," Carl said.

"What's that on your arms?" I noticed the familiar welts.

"I must have got into some stinging nettles when I was hiding," Little Donny said. "Man, does it itch."

"He's a hunted man," Carl said.

Carl could say that again. If the killer thought Little Donny got a good look at him, my grandson had more than the law after him.

FOURTEEN

Black bears are an integral part of life in the U.P. If anyone tells you we have grizzlies, don't believe them because it isn't true. If anyone tries to tell you how dangerous our bears are, don't listen to them. Unless, of course, you encounter a mama with her cubs.

Then you better run like . . . well . . . like you have a killer bear on your butt.

Fat chance of getting away, though, because our bears, in spite of their slow, clumsy gait, can outrun any human alive. And once they catch you, you're shredded cabbage.

That's what happened to BB Smith when he decided to wander away from his stinky bait pile to relieve himself against a Michigan conifer.

"Never, ever, leave your weapon behind," Walter said to him. "Why do you Detroit boys always have to learn everything the hard way?"

We were sitting around Walter Laakso's cluttered table, having ended the usual standoff in his yard.

"I survived, didn't I?" BB's bandaged arm hung in a sling and he bore several stitches closing the nasty gashes on his cheeks.

"And who do you have to thank for that?" Remy asked. "Me, that's who." Remy turned in my direction. "I heard him screaming and thrashing around in the bushes and so I came running. I didn't want to shoot at the bear because what if I hit BB instead? I didn't want to get too close in case she went for me, so I shot in the air a few times and she ran away."

Walter groaned. "Another thing I tell you over and over, practice shooting for hunting season before you get up here. What good does a rifle do if you can't hit what you shoot at?" He reached over to the counter and held up a coffee pot. "Gertie, how about some coffee? It's still hot."

I nodded and Walter poured some in a cup. It oozed out of the pot thick, like city sewer sludge, and it smelled old. He handed it to me.

"This calls for a little snort," he said, unscrewing the cap on a bottle of brandy and I wondered how many of Walter's

212

special occasions called for a shot or two. It seemed like every visit deserved an alcoholic toast.

I held a hand over my cup while Walter poured booze for the three brothers. Soon Marlin, Remy, and BB Smith would be running around in the backwoods, fired up on brandy, sporting weapons they couldn't shoot straight even when stone-cold sober.

That's life in the northern woods during hunting season.

"That bear cub was so cute," BB said, slurping brandy tinged with a splash of coffee. "Looked almost like a big furry puppy. I thought it was lost in the woods. Friendly little thing."

"Another hunting rule flushed down the toilet," Walter crabbed. "Never approach a bear cub, 'cause the mother bear is always someplace nearby."

"I've never seen such a *black* bear," Marlin said.

"That's why they call them black bears," Walter said, not bothering to hide the disgust in his voice.

"I saw one out west, it was brown," Remy said.

"Well, ours are black." Walter tasted his coffee and added more brandy.

"How's the stinging nettle, Walter?" I

asked, wondering how to ditch my cup of mud.

Walter rubbed his arm. "A little better. I spit on it as soon as I realized what happened and applied baking soda when I got home. That did the trick."

"It's odd that an old pro like you would get caught up in nettle."

"Happens to the best of us." We looked at each other. Walter grinned and I saw gaps in the front of his mouth where teeth used to be.

"Maybe you can show me where it is so I can look out for it," I fibbed. "I don't know what stinging nettle looks like."

"I'll show you as soon as we wrap up here."

Ordinarily at a pause in the conversation like this, we would have one of our traditional Yooper silences where we regroup and move on to another topic. But the Detroit boys weren't used to our ways, and the quiet bothered them. I could see them squirming, trying to think of something to keep the conversation going.

"Let's tell her about the warden," BB said, gleefully breaking the silence.

"Let's not," Marlin said, flatly, his coffee cup frozen in midair.

"Too late, blabbermouth," Remy said.

"She's not going to turn you in," Walter said. "She's one of us."

I looked over at Walter, sitting at his dirty table with brandy on his morning breath and no teeth in his head, and wondered when I became one of him. It must have snuck up on me so slowly while living all these years in the backwoods that I didn't notice until it was way too late.

But a private investigator is like an American Indian shapeshifter — mysterious, e . . . lusive, and able to blend in whenever she needs to. I decided to take Walter's comment as a compliment despite its potential to insult.

"Tell me what happened," I said to BB, remembering his words that first day I met him, something about a warden wanting to arrest him.

"They were shining way back by that last bait pile," Walter said. "And they got caught."

"Shining" involves hunting at night with spotlights, and it's illegal. Out-of-towners like to drive down our back roads after dark, piles of them stuffed into trucks, looking for good spots to shine their lights and take wild shots at startled animals. Unfortunately, our local warden, Rolly, rarely catches them.

I scowled for effect.

"I know," BB said, reading my face. "We shouldn't have been doing it and we didn't catch anything anyway so it doesn't matter. But we were sitting there by the bait pile minding our own business when we heard an ATV coming. We thought it was Walter so we didn't hide."

"Pretty soon the ATV stopped at the edge of our light," Remy said. "And we saw that it was a DNR agent and we were caught right there with the spotlight on our bait pile and rifles and no good excuse."

"We thought we were going to jail for sure," Marlin agreed.

"When was this?" I said.

"Real early in the morning when it was still dark, the same day that warden was killed."

I perked right up, and it wasn't because of the caffeine. The Detroit boys must have been the last to see Warden Hendricks alive, other than Little Donny and the killer in overalls.

"What did he look like?" I said.

BB shrugged. "He stayed in the shadows but he had on the clothes. You can't mistake that brown uniform for anything else."

"And he had a sidearm," Marlin added.

"And he talked real slow like John Wayne,"

BB added. "He said he was in a hurry to get somewhere but we should wait around and he'd be back to arrest us."

" 'Sit tight,' that's what he told us." Remy leaned over and said, confidential-like, "Yeah, right, like we'd wait there because he told us to. How dumb does he think we are?"

"Yeah," Marlin said, and added, "we came back to our trailer and hid the spotlight and went out again at dawn. But we stayed clear of that bait pile and we had our story worked out. It would be our word against his. Three against one. Later that morning we heard he'd been killed."

I shot a glance at Walter.

He could easily have followed the warden on his own ATV. And he had a motive. The warden had threatened three of his paying customers with jail time, and judging by the meagerness of his furnishings, Walter couldn't afford to lose the additional income.

"What do you think about all this?" I asked him, my eyes skimming over the stinging nettle welts on his arms.

"Bunch'a fuzzy fools," Walter said, kicking back from the table and mistakenly thinking my question was aimed at his guests rather than at the general situation. "Let's go. I'll show you the stinging nettle now."

"We're headed back out to hunt," BB said, and they all rose, draining the last dregs of coffee and brandy and gathering their equipment.

"Guess it's just you and me then." Walter gave me a toothless grin and picked up his sawed-off shotgun.

"Oh, look at the time," I said, feigning a glance at my watch. "I have to run. I'll take a rain check on that offer."

"In the meantime, watch where you walk," Walter said. "It's dangerous if you don't know what you're doing."

Studying his expressionless face, I couldn't decide whether or not I'd just been threatened.

I beat it out of there before the Detroit boys vacated the premises. No way was I going to get trapped alone with Walter.

I drove home, mulling over the new developments.

An experienced private investigator solves the crime through a process of elimination. I'd been practicing by solving sudoku logic puzzles in our local newspaper. They require patience and the ability to reason, using different variables and different patterns. Guessing and scribbling down a random number doesn't work in sudoku and it doesn't work in my business.

Once I locked on to Walter as a probable suspect, I went through the elimination exercise. Assuming Walter killed the warden to prevent him from arresting his current source of income (aka the Detroit boys), I was faced with some logistics problems. The most obvious involved the vehicles. If the warden rode one and Walter rode another, how did Walter get rid of the warden's ATV once he killed him? He couldn't ride both of them at the same time.

And I still couldn't explain how the warden had gotten himself into our woods when his truck was parked back in Marquette.

Did someone drop him off? If so, why didn't that person come forward? Warden Burnett said the ATV had been stolen. Why would Hendricks steal an ATV when he could take one anytime he wanted to?

Did the men come together?

Maybe one of the Detroit brothers helped Walter. That would take care of the ATV problem. The brother would have driven with Walter and moved the warden's ATV afterwards.

But Little Donny never mentioned a third person.

And the Detroit boys weren't the swiftest bunch. One of them would have slipped something incriminating to me today or to Cora Mae and Kitty when they double-dated. In spite of Cora Mae's hormonal imbalance and Kitty's turtle-like shuffle, both women were quick-witted and would have picked up on some inadvertent remark from a horny guy trying to impress a date.

Little Donny's accounting of the conversation between the killer and the warden about personal integrity and duty certainly pointed at Walter. He could have tried to talk the warden out of arresting the violators and killed him when he wouldn't back off.

Another troubling thought entered the equation. Little Donny had met Walter last year. Granted, it was a brief encounter, with my grandson taking a dive in the dirt when Walter beaded him with his shotgun. Also Walter had lost another tooth or two since then. But Little Donny should have recognized him.

He hadn't mentioned that.

If Walter really was our man, I'd wasted an entire week chasing bird feathers just because the dead man happened to have one stuck to his shoe.

Birds of a feather flock together.

I was about to follow that free-association thread of thought when I realized that I had driven all the way home without being aware I was even driving, proof that my skills were improving. I must have put the Trouble Buster on automatic and zoned out.

Fred jumped down from the truck on the lookout for the flock of guinea hens, off doing their business someplace else. After sizing up the house, which he knew was guarded by the old fly-whacker, he loped around the back where George was still working. Smart dog to choose George.

Heather was in the kitchen, looking a wreck since her son had vanished in the forest. She'd forgotten the basics of life like bathing, grooming, and sleeping.

I gave her a big hug and couldn't help whispering the good news about Little Donny in her ear. I hadn't planned to — I had decided *not* to tell her. It just bubbled over and spilled out before I could stop it up.

"He's alive?" she whispered back, searching my eyes for confirmation that she wasn't imagining our conversation. I nodded.

"It's our secret," I said. "You can't tell Blaze yet."

Heather clamped her hands over her mouth.

"You can't say anything to anyone," I repeated. "And you can't barrel over there either. Play it close to your chest until I have a chance to work this case through. Otherwise he'll be in a jail cell instead of the comfort of your Grandma's house."

I clamped my hand over my mouth. I *really* hadn't planned to tell her where he was.

She sat down hard on a kitchen chair and rocked back and forth, hugging her arms, while big buckets of tears ran down her face.

"Now what did you do?" Grandma Johnson said from behind me.

"She didn't do anything, Grandma," Heather said through the tears.

Grandma humphed. "You need to keep busy instead of weeping around all the time. What are we having for supper? Shouldn't somebody be starting it?"

"Chicken," Heather said, wiping her face with a handful of tissues. "I'm making chicken."

"Again? I'm not eating chicken four nights in a row." Grandma clacked her new teeth. "I made chicken the other day although nobody hardly ate any and we had it last night and in-between we eat chicken leftovers. I'm sick of it."

"I made pasties on Thursday," I reminded her. "There might be a few left we could heat up."

"Tasted like road rock." Grandma looked out the window, craning her neck. She swung her head around and beaded in on me with one cocked eyebrow. "I bet those guinea hens are good eaters."

"You leave my guineas alone," I demanded. In her day, Grandma was a sharpshooter in more ways than one. She had her rapid-fire snake tongue even back then, and she could really shoot a rifle. Chances are she'd lost her edge, but just to be sure, I thought about hiding her glasses.

"Once I find my pistol, I'm taking one of 'em down. Don't know how I could misplace it, but I'm on the lookout. It'll show up."

Annie Oakley shuffled off down the hall.

My home used to be my retreat from the world, but all that had changed.

These days I hated coming home.

FIFTEEN

My two partners ambled in, wearing their Sunday best, while I was listening to my police scanner and cleaning up the kitchen.

"Don't you look great," I said, standing back and taking in the sight. Cora Mae had on a pair of black stretch pants and a silver and blue camisole that should be illegal outside of a bedroom. Kitty wore blue jeans and a silver baseball cap emblazoned with a blue lion that was several sizes too small for her head. "Pin curls and ball caps. What'll they come up with next?"

"We're going over to Walter's to watch the game with the Smith brothers," Cora Mae said. "Want to come?"

"As tempting as that is, I have work to do." I'd rather eat Drano than spend the day warding off bacterial infection over at Walter's house.

"The Detroit Lions are playing the Green Bay Packers," Kitty said. "It's their first game together this year. I'm a closet Packer fan, though. It's going to be hard to cheer for the Lions."

"BB and his brothers are from Detroit. It's only polite," Cora Mae said. "It's Sunday, Gertie. No one works on Sunday."

"Maybe next time."

"We ran into Blaze at the gas station," Cora Mae said. "It's a shame they didn't find Little Donny in Newberry."

"I knew they wouldn't before Dickey and No-Neck left to go there," I said, feeling hurt that Blaze hadn't shared his recent findings with me. Instead he felt perfectly fine divulging police information to my friends. Then I remembered my big secret about Little Donny. I had no intention of confiding in Blaze, so I guess we were even.

Chatter erupted from my police scanner and we listened until we were sure it wasn't anything interesting.

"That detective and his partner drove by your house when we pulled in," Kitty said, helping herself to coffee. "Detective Dickey is a piece of work." She shook her head. "Nebbish."

"Bumptious," I agreed.

"An icky schmo," Cora Mae added, jumping into the contest.

"I'm your bodyguard," Kitty said to me.

225

"If you're working the case today, I'm coming along."

"I don't want to go to Walter's by myself," Cora Mae whined.

Heather trotted out of her room and I couldn't believe the transformation. She'd cleaned herself up, combed her hair, and applied make up. She had her purse in her hand.

"I'm going for groceries," she said. "Do you want anything special?"

I eyed her glowing face. "Only what we agreed on before," I said slowly, to remind her to stay away from Grandma Johnson's house. "You remember, don't you?"

"Oh, sure. Bye." And Heather bounced out, leaving me less than assured.

"Sit down," I said to Cora Mae and Kitty. "I have good news."

I told them about Carl and my suspicions and about finding Little Donny. Kitty jumped up and gave me a congratulatory embrace that almost cracked my ribs.

I broke free, or rather she released me, and I took a step back. In the north woods we don't go in much for public displays of affection, but Kitty tends to be dramatic, which is why I think she should become a lawyer and put all that pent-up energy to good use.

"Kitty, you have to stay with Cora Mae today," I said. "She might need protection more than I do."

I told them about the stinging nettle.

"You think Walter did it?" Kitty said. "It's possible that one or more of the Smith brothers could be in it, too. I see what you mean, Gertie, about being careful."

She glanced at Cora Mae. "We're sticking together as long as they're around."

I felt relieved. Kitty was a formidable opponent, both intellectually and physically. I didn't envy the fool who tried to cross her.

"We should stop by and say hi to Little Donny," Cora Mae said, standing up and stretching her lean legs.

"Stay away from Grandma's house," I said. "We don't want extra traffic on Porcupine Trail. Blaze isn't the brightest, but he might catch on. My plan is to solve this crime before he finds Little Donny."

The police scanner crackled into action, spitting static. "Code seven," someone said over the airwaves.

"That sounds like Blaze," Cora Mae said. "What's a code seven?"

"Lunch." I consulted my police radio manual. "He's out to lunch."

Kitty chortled and I grinned. "Out to lunch," she said. "That's a good one."

"Ten four," came another voice.

"The rest of the day is free and clear," I announced, sure that Blaze would flop on his couch for the Lions game and scarf down enormous bags of peanuts and multiple packages of pre-cooked brats.

Cora Mae wandered over to the window and I could tell she was getting antsy to go.

The police scanner crackled again and Blaze's voice came on. "Are you moving?"

"Code three," someone said.

"Geez, Deputy Sheedlo," Blaze complained for all to hear. "You have to study up on your codes. Code three is lights and sirens. Is that what you're trying to tell me? That you're in pursuit? I thought this was a routine observation."

"He's talking to No-neck," I said. "Dickey must be around someplace close, too."

"Yes, sir, affirmative, I will and no, sir, I'm not," No-Neck said. "I'll work on the codes. We're keeping our distance. Over and out."

Kitty clapped her hands. "I want one of these scanners. Where'd you get it?"

"Cora Mae gave it to me for my birthday."

"What's that yellow thing on your tire?" Cora Mae asked, still standing by the window.

"What yellow thing?" The three of us shoved our heads against the glass.

Everything in my yard looked normal. The hens were still in the outer field. Fred was sprawled in the grass, snoozing in the sun. I could hear George hammering away.

Everything looked the same as always except for my truck.

"What is it?" Kitty wanted to know. "Looks like some kind of yellow hubcap trim."

I knew exactly what it was because I've been scrutinizing the law enforcement buyer's guides I'd swiped from Blaze's house.

I'd seen a picture.

I shrieked and rushed outside. Kitty and Cora Mae were right behind. "How did he do this right under my nose?" I shouted. "He must have crawled up the driveway on his belly, the coward."

George appeared, holding a hammer loose in his hand. "I told him not to do it," he said. "But you know Blaze."

I kicked the tire.

"What is that thing?" Kitty repeated.

"A tire lock." I kicked it again with the other foot.

"She's been booted," George said.

"Look at this," Cora Mae called from the front of the truck. "A warning sticker. 'Warning,' it says. 'Your car has been immobilized. To arrange for removal, present the proper driving credentials and vehicle registration to your local sheriff.' "

I kicked the tire again, softer this time because the toes on both my feet were beginning to cramp up. "He can't do this right in my front yard. Doesn't he need a warrant to come on my property?"

"I'm making a few phone calls," Kitty said, lumbering for the house, sounding more like an attorney every day. "We'll know if he's within his rights in a minute."

"He's disowned," I said.

"You say that every time he does something that makes you mad," Cora Mae said.

"I mean it this time."

"You say that, too."

"These things are designed to intimidate you," George said. "It isn't absolutely foolproof, you know. I could get you back on the road in no time."

I calmed down when I considered that possibility. "Okay, let's do it."

"Wait for Kitty to research the law," George advised. "It's a criminal act to remove one. Blaze could arrest you." He smiled. "At least then I'd know right where you were and that you were safe."

I grinned back and ignored Cora Mae, who stuck her tongue out behind George's back, then put her finger in her mouth and pretended to gag.

Kitty marched out of the house like a woman on a mission. By her smug expression, I ventured a conclusion. "Illegal," I said.

"Right," Kitty said. "But if he catches you driving on the road or parked in town without the proper registration, he can clamp one on. Didn't you transfer the registration from your other truck? The one you rolled and totaled?"

"I haven't gotten around to it yet," I admitted. "George, how does it come off?"

George bent down. "If the jaws are loose, we can deflate the tire and slide the tire lock off." He shoved on the lock. "However, it's tight."

"Now what?" I said.

George glanced at Cora Mae. "You like tools, right?"

"Right," she agreed, rearranging herself into a sleazy pose.

"Get a chisel out of my toolbox. It's around the corner of the house. Gertie, do you have a spare tire for the truck?"

"Sure."

"I have to get to the lug nuts by taking off this plate." He pointed to a metal sheet clamped across the lug nuts.

Cora Mae sashayed off on her assigned mission, returned, and lingered over handing him the chisel. George went to work. He gave the tire lock several powerful strikes, while the three of us watched his muscles ripple. Another smack and a pin popped out. George jiggled this and that, then peeled the plate away, exposing the lug nuts. While he changed the tire, the Trouble Buster gang had a conference.

"You need to get over to Walter's house for the game," I said to my two cohorts. "Keep your eyes and ears open and don't get separated from each other. Ask a lot of questions and see what comes up."

Kitty and Cora Mae nodded in unison.

"Whatever you do, don't let Walter take you stinging-nettle hunting."

"Okay," Kitty said. "We'll stay together. What about you? If Blaze sees your truck on the road, he'll take it away permanently."

"I already thought of that after George started removing the lock," I agreed.

"Let him finish," Cora Mae said. "He likes to help. Right now you don't have any other way to get around, anyway."

"I have to find some other means of transportation," I said, chewing my lip. "Something nondescript to throw Blaze off my trail."

An idea formed.

I knew exactly where to find my interim wheels.

Little Donny's Ford Escort had been flat-bedded to the back of Ray's General Store, where it had joined a multitude of worn-out, broken-down beaters. They'd been collected over the years by our local law enforcement and its contracted towing service, owned by Ray and his son.

Ray, happy to have an additional source of income and unconcerned by the junk-yard appearance out back, also leased an outbuilding to the sheriff's department, just in case Blaze ever managed to nab a law-breaker needing temporary confinement.

Several local residents had occupied the establishment at one time or another, mostly binge drinkers who couldn't remember where they'd parked their cars and needed a place to bed down without freezing to death on the streets.

It had a holding cell with a cot and basic plumbing, and a little desk where Blaze could heft his feet for a snooze when he wanted the town to think he was actually working.

Deputy Dickey hadn't been able to drive Little Donny's car once he finished dusting for prints because I had the only key that started the car, and I wasn't about to raise red flags by handing it over.

Thus the tow.

After stopping at Ray's for several cans of black spray paint and a roll of duct tape, I parked my truck at the back of the junk heap where it couldn't be seen by anyone entering the makeshift jail. Then I crawled under Little Donny's car, ran a few strips of duct tape over the worst holes in the muffler to deaden some of the sound, and moved the car behind the junk heap a good distance from my new truck. I went to work.

I'd learned a few tricks about directional spraying from the mistakes I made on the Trouble Buster truck that used to belong to Blaze. But I couldn't worry too much about doing a perfect job. I was in a hurry. So if a little white paint showed through the black, I couldn't help it. Little Donny wouldn't be too happy about it, but if I got him out of his current pickle, he'd have to forgive me.

Less than an hour later, I pulled out of the back of Ray's General Store in my grandson's newly disguised car. I had to get used to the gear shifts all over again, but no one saw me stall out at the four-way stop. Everyone in Stonely had their eyes glued to the Lions and Packers football game. Other

than Herb's Bar, where the game was playing on an overhead television screen to a
lively crowd, the town was dead.

Sixteen

Once I mastered the clutch, I found myself driving toward Crevice Road. I couldn't get the "birds of a feather" phrase out of my head. A private investigator learns to trust her instincts, and mine were telling me to follow the flocking birds. Cora Mae and Kitty were checking out Walter and his paying guests, so I headed for the raptors.

Ted Latvala, falconer, red-tooth county resident and hostile gun-toter, had threatened to shoot me, so I planned to avoid him as much as possible rather than present myself again as a willing target.

I wished I had brought Fred along instead of sneaking out when his eyes were closed. I hadn't abandoned him altogether, though. Assuming that Grandma would get him if the guinea hens didn't, I'd left him in George's care with a firm promise from him to protect Fred from all directions and by any means necessary. George had also

236

agreed to move the Trouble Buster truck back to its spot in my driveway, with Carl's help, before Blaze noticed it missing.

Once on Crevice Road, I passed Latvala's house and pulled into the drive of the first house on the opposite side of the road. As I approached the house with my clipboard, I heard the game playing inside.

No one came to the door when I knocked.

I pounded until my hand hurt, then shuffled over to the window and peered in, my free hand cupped around my eyes to eliminate the glare.

I could see the game playing on a television. It looked like the Packers were ahead, but no one was in the room. After pounding one more time, I gave up and headed for the Ford.

The front door squeaked open as I was getting in, and a girl about seventeen peeked out. I hustled back and showed her my census identification and went through my introductory spiel.

"My parents are watching the game at someone else's house. You'll have to come back later," she said.

"You can answer the questions. They aren't hard."

A guy about her age walked past the door behind her with a guilty look on his face. I realized they were taking advantage of the absent parents and foregoing the football game for a more interesting sporting event.

In my opinion, kids need their parents more in their teens than when they were younger, and that's exactly the time parents think their jobs are done and stop paying close attention.

A ten-year-old has more common sense than four sixteen-year-olds put together. Hormones begin shooting every which way, and teenaged nervous systems malfunction, causing a loss of their reasoning abilities.

"Oh, I don't know," she said, hesitantly. "I'd rather not. I'm a little busy."

I bet. I decided to play my hunch.

"If you don't answer my questions, I'll have to find your parents and tell them." I managed a clear tone of implied threat and leaned to the left so I could stare behind her. "You wouldn't like that, would you?"

Her eyes shifted away. "No. I guess I wouldn't. What do you want?"

We went through the family basics and I wrote her answers down for effect. "Now," I said. "I need some information on your neighbor across the street."

"You can go over and ask them yourself," she said, beginning to close the gap in the door by a few inches. I edged my foot closer in case she tried to slam it. I never had so many doors slammed in my face as I have since landing this census job.

It's a good thing I have a thick skin and refuse to take rejection personally.

"Where did you say your parents were?" I asked, again looking behind her suggestively. Now I could add one more experience to my growing repertoire of private investigator tactics. Intimidating children.

We'll stoop to anything to solve a case.

"I don't know them," she answered, resigning herself. "They keep to themselves."

"How many people live over there?"

She shrugged. "I don't know. We just moved in last month."

"Do you notice anything odd about them?"

"Odd like how?"

"You know. Unusual."

"No. Can I go now?"

"What about his birds?"

"What birds?"

Reluctantly, I let her go back to whatever she was doing and spent the next ten minutes figuring out how to put Little Donny's beater in reverse. Every time I switched gears and eased my foot off the clutch, I jumped ahead another foot. The car was close to bumping up against the garage door when I finally found the proper gear and backed out of the driveway.

I had a livelier reception at the next house down Crevice Road.

"Come on in, Sweetheart, and meet Joe the Man." Joe the Man flattened himself against the wide-open door so I could enter. Then he leaned into me as I passed.

The leer on his face wasn't encouraging.

"It's halftime and the missus won't be home for another two hours," he said, staggering over and plopping down on a worn sofa. He patted the cushion next to him. "I can make all your dreams come true with time to spare."

Another leer. He had the unfocused eyeballs of someone who'd had one or two too many. The proof was scattered on the coffee table. I counted thirteen empty beer bottles, not including the one in his hand, and the game was only half over.

He patted the cushion again.

I sat on the arm of an easy chair instead and tried to look businesslike. I had my weapons purse slung over my shoulder and a pepper pen in the pen holder of my clipboard. It looked exactly like a pen but it was guaranteed to spray any target up to six feet away. There was a good chance I'd get to try it out today.

My next catalog order would include a pepper spray pager, designed to look exactly like a pager, but with enough *habaneros* pain-inflicting attacker-protection to stop a rhino dead in its tracks. It also had a clip included so it would attach to my purse or belt for easy access.

"Then I'll come over there by you," he said when I didn't move to join him. The beer must have settled in his bottom because he was having a tough time getting up from the sofa.

"No," I said, sharply, fingering the pepper pen and watching him sink back down. "First you have to answer questions."

"Ah, coy, are you? Okay. Bring 'em on." He leaned back, tipped the bottle, and took a long chug, then tried to focus on me with vacant eyes.

I decided to skip the census introduction and all the fake questions that preceded the real ones since my interviewee could pass out at any time.

"Tell me about your neighbor, Ted Latvala."

Joe the Man lost the thread of our conversation when the band finished marching across Ford Field and the second half of the game was about to begin.

"We better hurry, My Little Football," he

said. "We need to kick off."

His Little Football wasn't too worried. He'd never make it off the sofa.

"Ted Latvala." I raised my voice and spoke slowly. "What's he up to?"

"I should report him," Joe the Man blustered, refocusing, and working himself up. "Running a business out of his house without the proper license. Day and night. And the riffraff coming around . . ."

I'm sure Joe the Man could define riffraff for me on one of his sober days.

"What business? Falconry lessons? Target shooting? What?"

"Welding or something," he said. "They're at it in the back shed all night long. They don't even start till most of us are getting ready for bed. Sound carries out here and it drives me and the missus nuts."

"Welding?" I said. "Like soldering metal? Are you sure?"

"Clanging and . . ." He turned his attention back to the game. "Packers are going to lose this one. Oh. Oh. Look at that. Run. RUN," he screamed at the television set with more energy than I expected. Then he slumped back. "They deserve to lose playing like that."

My game was almost over, too. I'd lost Joe the Man to an alcoholic daze. "I have

242

all I need. Thank you for your time."

"Don't go yet. We're just getting started." He raised a limp arm in an attempt to grab me as I passed, but his timing was off and he fell sideways on the sofa.

"I have work to do," I said. "Start without me."

Warden Hendricks had died with a bird feather in the tread of his shoe and a red bear tooth lying nearby. None of my favorite private investigators on television would have ignored those clues. Maybe birds and bears tied in with Walter and the Detroit boys, and maybe they didn't, but I had to follow them to their natural conclusion. Only after eliminating them as possibilities would I be able to move on.

Which led me to Ted Latvala.

I wasn't thrilled at the prospect of dodging buckshot spray, but I had one more thing to do before going home.

I was wearing my running shoes and dark clothes, and they'd blend into the tree line. I left my orange cap and jacket in Little Donny's car and reluctantly decided that my weapons purse would slow me down. I tucked the pepper pen in my pocket, threw the purse on the floor, and left the Escort parked in Joe the Man's driveway.

I had at least an hour before his wife would return. More than enough time for a quick surveillance run without the missus discovering a strange car in the drive. I figured the football game would provide enough entertainment at Latvala's to keep him busy so I could slip in and out undetected.

I walked down the road without encountering any passing cars, I slid into the pines along his driveway, cut into the woods, and tromped through the bramble until I came to the back of his house. Four outbuildings loomed ahead, close together, three of them sheds and one larger building behind those. They were my targets.

The noise of cheering televised football floated on the air.

I noted several pickup trucks in the driveway, along with the same pile of scrap vehicles I'd seen the first day of our fiery acquaintance. I stopped behind the first shed with my heart thumping in my chest and beads of nervous perspiration on my forehead. I concentrated on regular heartbeats, and when I got my nervous system under control, I peeked through a small window.

I spotted a tractor, a lawnmower, and a snowmobile. Nothing useful.

I'd have to check the next building, and that meant a pass right through the back-yard in full view of the house. I held my breath, stilled my beating heart, and ran across the yard, stopping behind the shed-like building.

Nothing from the house. No movement anywhere and no sound other than the game. I pressed my ear against the building and listened.

I heard male voices close by and flattened tightly against the outer wall.

The Packers must have scored because I heard hooting and clapping. The game was playing right inside the building next to my head — not in the house.

Just great.

Couldn't they watch the game in the house like everybody else? Who hangs out in a shed during a football game?

I rifled through my options. Although the best choice seemed to be running away as fast as I could, my curiosity wouldn't let me. I scooted along the small building, crouched under a window on the far side of the commotion, and forced myself to look through the dirty pane.

I fastened my eyes on the back side of three scruffy characters, all riveted to the game's action on the other side of the room.

A commercial break began, and instead of using the time to pop open another beer like most men would, they went to work.

Joe the Man had been right about the welding. One of them clamped a welding hood on his head and flames shot from a torch in his hand. While the others watched, he attacked a piece of pipe on a workbench and sparks flew.

I saw piles of steel and iron rods and metal gizmos everywhere. I have to confess that I know nothing about welding gadgets and equipment, but whatever these guys were making, it seemed like I'd stumbled onto a hobby group sharing a common metal-working interest.

This surveillance run hardly seemed worth risking buckshot in my back end.

I pulled a piece of tissue out of my pocket and dabbed it on a corner of the window, hoping to clear away a little dirt for a better view.

A piercing wail sliced the clear September air. The window must have been set up with an intrusion detector. Dang.

The members of the innocent hobby club jerked to attention and looked at each other. The one with the welding hood pulled it off, and I could see Ted Latvala reaching for a rifle propped against the wall. He handed it to the welder and grabbed another rifle for himself.

The rifles triggered a response from me.

I can handle tangling with a shotgun. You stand a chance of surviving buckshot, even a direct hit. But if Latvala's aim was as accurate as most Yoopers and he got a bead on me through his rifle's scope, I'd never make it to the pines alive.

I'd been on the receiving end of weapons before. Whenever Walter drew on me, I didn't flinch, knowing he did that to all his visitors until they identified themselves. But something told me these men might be dead serious about silencing trespassers, and I didn't want to stick around and test the strength of my instincts.

I ran to the third building, yanked open the door, and rushed inside. Wings beat me in my face and something alive headed out the same door I'd decided to hide behind.

I closed it as quietly as I could and turned to squint into the dark. The only light came from two small windows. My eyes adjusted quickly to the gloom, and I didn't like what I saw.

I faced a shed full of birds. Not cute little yellow canaries or colorful chirping parakeets like my kids had when they were young. These were enormous, hooked-

beaked, razor-clawed carnivores with staring, beady eyes. I hoped they'd been fed
recently.

They were everywhere.

"Shhh . . . ," I said to them, moving
stealthily to test the back window, not finding any way to open it. I plastered myself
against the wall, pepper pen clutched in my
fist, trapped.

Nobody inside the bird house moved.
Other than the escapee, no one's feathers
seemed ruffled that I had crashed their hen
party. One bird bobbed its head in my direction.

"What happened?" I heard someone say
outside.

"Turn off the alarm before the entire
neighborhood hears it. That's all we need. A
bunch of nosy neighbors."

The alarm went silent.

"Anybody see anything?"

"I'll check around the house. You go that
way."

Silence.

The birds didn't blink. All eyes were on
me.

"For crying out loud. One of the birds is
loose," I heard Latvala say. "How many
times do I have to tell you to be careful
when you open the coop door?"

248

"I didn't do it."

"Me, neither."

"That's the same one that makes a run for it every single time it gets a chance."

"What a pain."

"How are we going to get it out of the tree?"

"Forget the bird," Latvala said. "It'll show up tonight when we feed the rest. Check the perimeter. The alarm went off for a reason."

"I think the bird hit the window and triggered the sensors."

"I didn't hear a thud."

"The game was pretty loud. So was the welding."

I squeezed my eyes shut and held my breath. The last voice that spoke was directly outside. My head must be three inches from his. I had my trusty pepper pen, but it wasn't going to buy me much time against three scoped weapons.

If I had to use the spray, I would take out Ted Latvala first and hope for the best with the other two.

Even through the terror I felt at the moment, I had enough presence of mind — like the detective I am — to wonder why they had intrusion detectors installed on the windows if they were members of a friendly little welding club.

If they were up to no good and really were selling illegal hunting birds, shouldn't the building that housed the birds be the one with intrusion protection? No alarm went off when I opened the coop door or when I touched its back window, so I had to assume it was alarm free.

What were they making in the other outbuilding that warranted a security system?

A shadow fell across the inside of the coop and I knew someone was peering through the window. I stretched as thin as I could against the wall and promised not to eat another sugar doughnut for the rest of my life if I made it out of here.

The shadow moved past.

"Maybe you're right," Latvala said. "Fool bird. Let's get back to work. I promised the next shipment would go out late tomorrow morning."

They moved away.

I didn't budge for a full fifteen minutes. I hadn't checked the largest outbuilding but my courage was failing me. The birds continued to stare me down. The floor was covered in bird doo-doo. I lifted a running shoe and glanced at the bottom.

My eyes were adjusting to the darkness.

Birdie doo-doo and little feathers stuck to the bottom of my shoe.

I had found Warden Hendricks' last stop before he was murdered at Carl's bear bait pile.

But I didn't know what to do with that information or whether or not it was relevant.

I slunk out the same way I came in, with a pounding heart and a hopeful attitude.

By then Blaze had arrested Little Donny for murder one.

SEVENTEEN

"I told you to stay away from Little Donny," I said, while slamming bowls onto the table. "What part of 'stay away from Grandma's house' didn't you understand?"

Heather boohooed like she always does when life turns upside-down and she can't handle it. "I didn't think it would hurt," she sobbed.

"Blaze and his cronies were yakking about you on the police scanner and I didn't figure it out. It went right over my head. Dickey Snell and No-Neck Sheedlo were following you." I slammed another bowl. "You led them right to him."

Boohoo, snort, blow.

"Using my house as a hideout!" Grandma exclaimed, leaning on the back of a chair for support. "Is that what you're saying? Right under my nose, too. We need to go over and see if those roughnecks busted it up."

"The house is fine," I said. "Don't you care at all about what's happening to Little Donny?"

"What about Little Donny?" Grandma asked, her teeth snapping and her scrawny turkey neck craned in my direction. "Is he finally coming to visit? It's about time. I haven't seen him for over a year."

"Never mind," Heather said to her, patting Grandma's wrinkled, liver-spotted hand. "Everything is going to be fine."

"What are we having to eat?" Grandma asked, sitting herself down at the table and picking up her spoon.

"Canned soup," I said. "Soup and crackers."

"As long as it isn't chicken."

I ladled chicken noodle soup into her bowl and threw a package of saltine crackers into the center of the table.

How was I supposed to solve the warden's murder and plan meals, too? I was running surveillance, almost getting myself killed on top of it, and I was supposed to put food on the table for two helpless, basket-case women. Heather had to pull herself together and help out or Grandma would show up at the stove again, expecting to cook, and end up poisoning us all.

"What happened over there?" I asked

Heather.

Grandma slurped her soup. "What kind of soup is this?"

"Tuna," I answered. "And let Heather talk."

"That vicious dog of yours is back," Grandma said. "Heather tied it up behind the house until the dogcatcher can come and haul it away."

Heather shook her head at my questioning look. "George dropped Fred off right before you came home. He's out back. I thought it was safest."

"Will you please tell me what happened," I repeated.

"The skinny deputy tried to kick in grandma's door, but it didn't work. Then the other one, the big wrestler-like one, smashed out a window and pushed his gun through and yelled that we were under arrest."

"What was wrong with knocking on the door?"

"Blaze asked the same thing. It wasn't locked and Little Donny wasn't armed but they didn't even check to see if it was open. They could have walked right in. But the skinny one got excited when his partner broke the window and he shot through the door, almost hitting me. Blaze is mad. He made them put plastic over the window and

254

they have to pay to have everything re-paired."

"Dickey never had any brains," I said.

"Dickey Snell?" Grandma piped up, hunched over her bowl of soup, the spoon halfway to her mouth. "Is that the same Dickey Snell who shot Blaze in the back with a pellet gun when they were young?"

"The same one," I agreed.

"Never liked that kid," she said.

"Blaze says his deputies are coming around first thing in the morning to take our fingerprints," Heather said.

"Why would they do that?"

"Blaze and Deputy Snell think Little Donny has an accomplice and they're try-ing to eliminate friendly prints. Blaze also said Little Donny's car is missing."

"Little Donny would still be safe at Grand-ma's if I didn't have such a big mouth," I said to Cora Mae over the phone. "I never should have told his mother. What was I thinking?"

"It isn't your fault," Cora Mae said. "You did your best."

I related my afternoon adventure playing war games at the Latvala camp and she gasped and clucked sympathetically in all the appropriate pauses.

"I keep thinking I'm missing something," I said. "I can't understand why anybody would need to commit murder over a bunch of birds or over a little night poaching. There's more at stake here than we think. Call Kitty. Both of you need to pick me up first thing tomorrow. Latvala's sending the next shipment, whatever that means. Let's intercept it."

"What about Walter? I thought you said he did it?"

"The problem is, we have too many suspects and we have to start eliminating them. It still certainly could be Walter. What did you find out at the game?"

"Not much. The Lions won but it was close. In the last thirty seconds . . ."

"Not the *game*, Cora Mae. You were supposed to interrogate the Smith brothers and keep an eye on Walter."

"BB repeated the story about the warden catching them shining, but he didn't say anything new."

"I was hoping for a more detailed description."

"Other than the warden's foreign accent, he —"

"What foreign accent?" I interrupted.

"BB thought he might be from down south, Arkansas or Georgia. Maybe from

Denmark or New Jersey."

"Cora Mae," I said, disgusted. "Which is it? None of those accents are remotely the same."

I didn't know what a Dane sounded like, but I was pretty sure I wouldn't confuse the accent with a Georgian's or a New Joisey-en's.

"That's what he said. I'm just repeating it."

"Was he drinking?"

"Not a drop. Well, maybe one. Has George been around?"

"He went on vacation," I lied. "You better concentrate your efforts on BB."

"When will George be back?"

"Just get over here first thing tomorrow before Dickey shows up with his fingerprint-ing kit."

The capture of the local sheriff's alleged serial-killer nephew sent every resident in three counties charging over for a look. It also revved up both the Escanaba and the Marquette news media, and they raced from opposite ends of the U.P. for exclusive live coverage. The news vans hovered around Ray's General Store like one giant collective buzzard hunting for scraps of Little Don-ny's flesh. Meanwhile, Blaze's deputies held off potential trouble with a visible array of police batons and a lot of verbal threats.

It was ten at night before I arrived at the jail, but the glow of the media's lighting systems illuminated the moonless sky for miles in every direction, reminding me of how the sky looks in a big city.

I parked Little Donny's newly painted Ford Escort down near the four-way stop and walked up the road with Fred on a leash. Blaze came out of his office as I arrived. When all the camera lights swung in his direction, I assumed this was the first action the media had seen.

"This isn't going to turn into a free-for-all," I heard Blaze shout, although I couldn't see him. The mass of bodies with cameras and notebooks drew together tighter. I surveyed the crowd and noticed that Blaze had deputized more of the local residents than usual, and they were taking their new positions seriously.

Someone was bound to get shot before the end of the night.

"Now," his voice continued. "Deputy Snell is here to take questions and then I want you all to go home. This is my town and I won't have it overrun like this. Deputy Snell?"

Dickey leaped up in the bed of a pickup

truck so everyone could see him. He held both arms high over his head like he was the president of the United States greeting his constituents from the steps of Air Force One. "As you know, we apprehended the alleged suspect at seventeen hundred hours at an undisclosed location. It quickly became a dangerous hostage situation."

I shook my head. From my understanding, the only thing dangerous about the apprehension was Deputy Dickey.

"I'm going to give you some information," he said, "but I won't be answering questions so listen up. And you reporters, write fast because I'm not repeating myself." He cleared his throat importantly. "I and Deputy Sheedlo cornered the suspect in his hideout. A fight ensued, we managed to subdue the alleged party in question, and he's incarcerated here temporarily. The hostage was unharmed. The prisoner will be moved to a more secure facility tomorrow so you can all rest easy later. But for tonight, keep your firearms handy."

Thanks to Fred's ability to scare people, I had worked my way closer.

Blaze, looking like he'd swallowed tacks, rushed over and displaced Dickey. "That's enough. Thank you for the colorful rendition, Deputy Snell, but everyone can forget

259

the need for weapons. The suspect turned himself in willingly and no force was even close to necessary. There was no hostage taken. We'll have guards stationed but we aren't expecting any trouble."

The reporters, who had been scribbling madly while Dickey told his story, didn't take a single note of Blaze's attempt at rectifying the tall tale.

I could see tomorrow's headlines already. *Relative of Local Sheriff Runs Amok and Is Taken Down Like Rabid Dog.*

Anybody who wasn't here tonight would think the story was about me.

Blaze stormed into his office, and the deputies tried to restore order. I crept around the back of the crowd with Fred leashed at my side. Surprisingly, my companion was walking like he'd been trained to heel instead of ripping out my arm socket as he usually did.

It was a good thing George and Carl moved my truck from behind the junk heap before the commotion started or I'd have a lot of extra explaining to do. Speaking of . . .

"Carl," I called to a familiar figure ahead of me. He turned around and I saw the shining badge. "What's up?"

"Blaze deputized me," he said, proudly.

"Does he know you helped Little Donny hide?"

"Holy smokes, Gertie, keep your voice down."

"Sorry." I swung my gaze around to see if anyone had overheard. "Thanks for moving my truck," I said, softer.

"You're going to get me in all kinds of trouble before this is over. I shouldn't have helped George with your truck."

Carl sounded like Grandma Johnson.

"You're doing a fine job of finding trouble without my input," I reminded him.

"I tell ya, I don't know if I'll ever hunt again." Carl's eyes shifted to study the crowd. "For sure I'm not going back to my bait pile. I keep seein' all that blood in my mind."

"You'll be just fine."

"Are you going to snitch on me for helping Little Donny?"

"I tell you what. You get me through this mob and into the jail, and your secret goes to the grave with me."

"Deal," Carl said, shifting his eyes up and down and sideways. "But Blaze won't like it."

"I want to be deputized," I said to Blaze, who sat at his desk with his feet crossed over a stack of jumbled papers.

Fred, standing level with the desk, slid his big, black head next to Blaze's shoes and sniffed.

"I don't know how you got in here," he said, eyeing the entrance. Carl had taken off like a jackrabbit heading for his hole with a coyote after him. "But you need to go back home."

"Hi, Little Donny," I called out to a massive body lying on a cot inside the cell.

"He's sleeping," Blaze said, swinging his feet down. "How he can sleep with all the excitement outside is beyond me." He flipped his sheriff's hat onto the desk and rubbed his face roughly with both hands as though he was erasing a bad dream.

"He's innocent, you know," I said. "All he's guilty of is eating day-old bakery and sleeping in the woods."

"I'd like to believe that, but he won't talk to me. He zipped up his lip and the only thing he's asked for is food."

Good for Heather and her city-smart fancy husband, Big Donny. She must have told him to clam up until they could get a lawyer in to see him.

"You're keeping him here, I hope," I said. "Near his family until this is cleared up."

Blaze shook his head. "He's headed for

Escanaba tomorrow where they have a real jail and more security."

"He isn't a flight risk."

Blaze glanced at me. "He's been running all along."

Good point. Hard to argue against firm facts.

"But," Blaze said, "I'm doing it for his own protection. Billy Lundberg might have been the town drunk, but his family goes way back and people are riled up."

A deputy came in and saluted. "Most everybody has gone home," he reported. "Even the news trucks are packing up for the night. What should we do now?"

"Tell the deputies we need two guards around the clock," Blaze said. "The rest are on call in case I need them."

"Aye, aye, sir."

"They all think they're United States Marines," Blaze complained when the deputy marched out. "Saluting and aye, ay-ing."

"Well?" I said.

"Well, what?"

"Am I a deputy?"

"No, Ma, you're not."

I pointed in the general direction of the street and I felt my face getting hot. "Onni Maki's out there flashing a badge through all those gold chains around his neck. If he can do a deputy's job, anybody can."

"Onni really is an ex-Marine."

"If Billy Lundberg wasn't dead you'd deputize him. You'd rather have a drunk than your own mother."

"That isn't true."

"I didn't see one woman deputy. How do you explain that? This is sex discrimination."

Blaze stared at me. "You're exaggerating, as usual. I'm not deputizing you because you'd think that was your signal to run totally wild. You don't have much restraint as it is."

"What's that supposed to mean?" I demanded, hands on hips.

Fred sat down with a plunk as our tones shifted, and his ears flattened against his head. Obviously he didn't like conflict any more than I did.

"Go home, Ma."

"A warden riding an ATV caught Walter's hunting guests shining bear."

"So? Out-of-towners get caught breaking the law all the time."

"It happened the same morning Hendricks was killed, and Walter has stinging nettle welts on his arms just like Little Donny. He could have killed the warden for threatening to arrest the Detroit boys. Or one of those boys could have eliminated Hendricks."

"Assuming your theory is right, which it isn't, how do you explain the arrows in Billy's back?"

"Mistaken identity. Billy Lundberg was killed because he was wearing Little Donny's cap. My grandson saw the murderer."

"Well, he's safe in here," Blaze said, dismissing me with a wave. "Maybe tomorrow Little Donny will open up and tell me his side of the story."

"I'm warning you," I said, with a menacing glare. "Nothing better happen to Little Donny. I'm holding you solely responsible for his safety."

"Nothing's going to happen to him."

"Someone in Maple County is dealing in illegal birds. Don't you want to know about that?"

Blaze stood up slowly and towered over me while he attempted to hitch his pants over his protruding stomach. He puffed his chest out and a button zinged past.

Blaze's intimidation tactics never worked on me. I poked him hard in his extended midsection. He let out a puff of air and his brashness deflated significantly.

"Little Donny didn't do it," I said.

"Prove it," Blaze said, sounding like a child.

That's exactly what I planned on doing. I'd exonerate Little Donny and drag the real killer in by his shorts. Or rather, Fred, the private eye dog, could handle the back-end work.

Tomorrow I'd pin on my new sheriff's badge and turn this town upside-down until I found the truth and the real killer.

Deputized by the local sheriff or not.

EIGHTEEN

Dickey and No-Neck banged on the door before the sun crested the top of the pines. I still wore my robe and hadn't poured my first cup of coffee yet.

A roving band of guinea hens pecked at their ankles as I peered out the window, re-affirming my birds' ability to sift through the dirt and find the biggest insects.

No-Neck had a big box under his arm.

I opened the door just enough for Fred to stick his head out. I considered siccing Fred on them to assist the hens, but after sniffing his former law-enforcement colleagues, Fred plunked down and concentrated on licking his paws.

"Ow," Dickey said, raising a leg. "Let us in. What's wrong with these birds?"

I wanted to say that the birds knew fools when they encountered them. Instead I said, "You can't come in. Tell Blaze that."

"He authorized us to use reasonable force,

if necessary," Dickey said, with a militant gleam in his eyes. "He warned us about you. We know you're hostile to law enforcement and to rules and regulations."

"What's going on?" Grandma Johnson mumbled from behind me. She didn't have her teeth in yet and it wasn't a pretty sight.

"Blaze's deputies want to fingerprint all the members of our family," I said.

"Over my dead body," Grandma said. "You young puddle-jumpers aren't telling me what to do." She waved a scrawny finger at the deputies.

"We don't need your prints, ma'am," Dickey explained. "Blaze said you haven't vacated the premises for weeks so yours aren't required."

"Well, that's different. Come on in," Grandma said. "I suppose you're after Gertie." She gave me the evil eye. "Figures she'd be involved in something bad."

I didn't know what to do. If I let them take my fingerprints and Blaze discovered that I'd been driving Little Donny's car, he might arrest me just to keep me out of the way. That's one man who hates professional competition and will do anything to quell it, even if it means jailing his own mother.

If I refused, these two clowns would be on my tail all day and I wouldn't be able to work the case.

Then I had an idea. An old idea but newly remembered.

"What are you waiting for?" I said, backing up into Grandma. "Let's get this over with. The coffee's almost ready by now."

Everyone stepped gingerly around Fred.

No-Neck placed his box on the table, opened it, and started sifting through the equipment while I set a heaping plate of home-made sugar doughnuts on the table.

"Let me change out of my robe," I said, palming a tube of super glue from my trusty junk drawer. "I'll be right back."

I changed as quickly as possible, then pierced the tube with a needle and ran a thin layer of super . . . glue across the fingers of my left hand, being extremely careful not to touch them together. I'd done *that* once, by accident, before I discovered that polish remover would unglue them. That time I ended up at the Escanaba hospital.

I've been there, done that, and since I didn't have any polish remover in the house, I wasn't taking chances. After waving my fingers around and blowing on them until they dried, I did the same thing to the fingers of my right hand.

With any luck, the glue would fill in the whorls in my fingertips and I'd beat Blaze at his own game.

I wondered if anyone had ever tried this before.

"They don't need Heather's prints either, since she arrived after your shenanigans," Grandma said to me when I returned to the kitchen. She was in the process of pouring coffee for the deputies, but most of it missed the cups, puddled on the countertop, and ran down the cabinets.

Dickey Snell stood formally, awaiting my return, but No-Neck had a sugar doughnut in each hand, and his cheeks were packed like a squirrel stowing it away for the first snowfall. Dickey was too anal-retentive to expose his human side, but I caught him glancing longingly at the heaping plate.

"There," Grandma said, sloshing the half-filled cups in front of them. "You can fancy it up yourself. Cream and sugar's on the table." She pulled out a chair and sat down. "Can you take that dog off our hands?" she asked Dickey. "It's going to bite somebody's leg off."

"The dog stays," I said.

"Suit yourself. It's your house. But the thing is vicious. I'm surprised it hasn't eaten all the guineas yet. It's going to bite some-one and you'll be facing a lawsuit. Probably lose everything you have." She glanced around the room and humphed. "Not that you have anything worth keeping. Barney's turning in his grave for sure."

I tried not to look at Grandma's sunken toothless mouth.

Dickey strutted around the room like a rooster, wearing his green, cat-hair-crusted jacket. My cat allergy kicked in and I started sneezing. "You'll have to wait outside," I told him between sneezes. "I'm allergic to you."

He frowned, and I could see he was thinking about protesting. After several more violent sneezes directed his way, he reconsidered. "I'll be outside," he said to No-Neck. "Shout if you need me."

No-Neck nodded and picked up my wrist. "I'm going to roll your fingers one at a time. Try to relax."

Grandma Johnson watched the procedure with great fascination. "Keep me posted when you get the results," she said. "I need to know what kind of person I'm living with."

Five minutes later the deed was done. No-Neck packed up his equipment and the two deputies disappeared down the road, leaving angry guinea hens in their Chevy dust.

I called Cora Mae and asked her to bring over a bottle of nail polish remover when she and Kitty picked me up. After that I sorted through my weapons purse to make sure it was fully loaded.

Today was the day I'd solve the crime. I felt it deep in my bones the same way I feel a gathering thunderstorm.

"Where are you going?" Grandma shouted as I slid into the back seat of Kitty's rusted-out Lincoln. Fred bounded across the yard, leaped over my lap, and settled next to me, his tongue hanging almost to the floor.

"Here and there," I shouted back.

"Billy Lundberg's funeral is starting at nine o'clock," she said, shuffling toward Kitty's car. She had her purse in her hand and her best hat on her head. "Drop me at Ed Lacken's Funeral Home in Trenary. Heather will pick me up if you can't bring me back."

"Have Heather take you," I suggested.

"She's moping in her room and won't get dressed."

"I forgot all about the funeral," Cora Mae said from the passenger seat. "We should stop in and pay our respects, too."

"We have something important to do," I said. "The interception, remember? We aren't going to Trenary."

Ed Lacken operated the only funeral home in our area. Everybody used him. My husband, Barney, and all three of Cora Mae's deceased husbands had been done up by Ed.

Grandma eyed Fred. "Get that mutt out of the car."

"He's coming along," I said, hoping that would dissuade her.

Kitty started the car and revved the engine. "Trenary's on the way. We can stop in for a minute. Hop in."

Grandma couldn't decide if a ride next to Fred was worth the effort or not. Then she slid in, wary and alert for trouble.

She should have been more worried about the car's driver.

Just as she closed the car door, Kitty ripped out of the driveway. Grandma slid across the seat against Fred, and Fred plowed into me. We all piled up on my side in a bunch of flailing arms and legs.

Grandma smelled like cheap perfume and dentures, and Fred smelled like . . . well . . . like ripe dog. If I ever smell like either of them, I'll expect Cora Mae to put me out of my misery.

"Holy cripes," Cora Mae said at the next turn.

"Holy mackerel," Grandma yelled, trying to straighten herself up and get away from her canine nemesis. "Where's the fire?"

Fred, sensing Grandma's discomfort and wanting to help, licked her face, one long, dead-on slurp. Once she recovered from the assault, she hit him with her purse and wiped her face with her sleeve. "Worthless," she muttered. "The whole bunch."

I imagined I was at the top of the worthless bunch list, although Fred might have notched past me into first place.

We got to the funeral home in breakneck time. For once in her life, Grandma didn't spew a continual stream of verbal abuse. She gripped the seat with white knuckles and her cheeks were sucked together like she'd licked a lemon. When we stopped, she crawled out and examined Kitty's car. "That was some race car driving," she said, straightening her hat. "Don't bother waiting for me. I'll find another ride home. I'd rather walk than go through that again."

She shuffled off, wobbling slightly.

"I thought you told me George was out of town," Cora Mae said when she spotted his truck in the parking lot.

"He must have decided to come back early," I said, watching her jump out of the car. She hurried into the funeral home, actually elbowing past Grandma in her haste and almost bowling the old prune over.

What was I going to do to keep Cora Mae and her Wonderbra'd boobs away from George?

"Two minutes and then we leave," I said to Kitty. "We don't want to miss the action."

"What are we looking for?" Kitty wanted to know, hefting herself out from behind the steering wheel.

"I'm not sure exactly. We'll know it when we see it. Latvala promised someone a shipment of something and that sounds big."

Kitty gave me a piercing look. "Okayyyyy," she said, doubtfully.

"I didn't get a chance to check his largest outbuilding before the alarm went off. I'm guessing it contained a white moving van."

Fred had his nose plastered against the car window and a dejected, poor-me ear tilt. The howling would commence the minute we vanished from sight. I could tell.

"I know," I said, always pleased when I thought of a solution. "We'll take turns going in. It'll take longer, but that way, Fred won't flip out. One of us can stay out here and watch the road in case a moving van goes by."

"Good idea," Kitty said. "You go first. I'll stay with Fred."

"I'll make it quick. If you see anything suspicious, lay on the horn and I'll run out."

Funerals are big in the U.P. Weddings, funerals, and senior citizen potlucks are our main sources of entertainment and they draw quite a crowd. Ed Lacken's parking lot was jammed full. Although we'd had to park farthest from the funeral home we were closest to the road. Perfect placement for a stakeout.

Best of all, I hadn't seen Blaze's sheriff truck, which meant he was watching his ward like he should be. I didn't think he'd get around to moving Little Donny until later in the day. Blaze wasn't exactly a high-octane performer. He'd take his sweet time, which I was counting on.

I hustled into the funeral home.

George met me in the hallway. I scanned the locals gathered in the green room without spotting Cora Mae.

"She's on the other side by the casket smelling the flowers," George said, as though reading my mind. "I managed to slip away. That woman's like a wood tick."

He grinned as we walked in together.

"I only have a few minutes," I said. I'd missed George's company. My new investigation business was threatening to consume all my time. I smiled to realize that now I actually had a personal life to occupy me after spending the last few years deep in mourning. "In a day or two," I said, feeling awkward but determined to spit it out, "maybe we can sit down someplace quiet and work on my written driving test."

I saw Cora Mae pushing her way over.

"I'd like that," he said, following my gaze and tensing. "Gotta go. I'll be over to work on the sauna later and we can talk." He gently squeezed my arm in farewell.

George faded into the crowd and Cora Mae abruptly changed direction like she had a Global Positioning System unit lodged in her bosom.

Surveying the mourners, I saw Dickey and No-Neck and several of Blaze's other newly-sworn deputies. Shouldn't these so-called law-and-order protectors be surrounding my grandson to keep him safe? Instead, they lounged around, waiting for the snacks to come out after the funeral.

Onni Maki shouldered by, his hair wrapped over his bald spot, a pinky ring on his little finger, his eyes focused on Cora Mae. They'd dated briefly — but Cora Mae has dated every man in the county at one time or another and her territory was widening.

I thought about offering to pay Onni to distract her from George, but rejected the idea as pathetic.

Grandma Johnson had joined a group of old battle-axes just like her. They huddled in a gossipy circle, an assortment of outdated hats and flowery handbags, with every single one of their mouths wagging simultaneously. I could only hope today's hot topic didn't involve me.

I made my way to the casket for my last look at Billy. He'd spent years bellied up to the bar at Herb's, never causing a ruckus or uttering an unkind word. He was like background music you didn't really hear until someone turned it off. Then you noticed the silence. Most of us could remember back before the booze got him when he still had a wife and kids who would speak to him.

Standing by the casket, I reflected on his life. Then my thoughts turned, as they always did at times like this, to my Barney and our time together.

I knew exactly what the families of Billy Lundberg and Robert Hendricks were going through with their unexpected losses. After Barney drowned in his waders in the Escanaba River, I didn't think I could go on without him.

Everybody has secrets and mine came back to me while standing in Ed's funeral home next to Billy's casket. When Barney died, I told everyone he had a massive heart attack while fishing, but that wasn't true. Blaze and Cora Mae are the only ones who know the truth about the drowning.

Barney, expert fisherman and all-around sportsman, wouldn't have wanted to go out with an embarrassing splash, so I concocted my own ending.

The old familiar pain of loss shot through deep inside of me and I shook it off by telling myself I'd have time later to let memories overtake me. Right now, there was work to do.

The Detroit boys walked in as I was leaving. They'd slicked their hair down with something greasy for the occasion and they'd shaved away the hunting growth accumulated in the backwoods. I noticed that they cleaned up well.

After a quick greeting, I got right to the point. "Where's Walter?"

"He visits his brother every Monday morning," Remy said.

"Like clockwork," BB said.

My ears perked up at this because the warden was killed last Monday morning. "I didn't know he had a brother."

"He's in a nursing home in Escanaba," Remy explained. "Walter never misses the visit. He left before seven o'clock to have breakfast with him. After that they play poker with a group in the home."

"Walter said he hasn't missed one of their card games since his brother went in," BB said. "And he wasn't going to miss today even for Billy's funeral. He said anybody that dies drunk, dies happy, and there isn't any need to cry over it."

That sounded just like something bourbon-brained old Walter would say.

"Tell me about the warden's accent," I said, switching gears. I'd ponder the new information later. "You didn't say a word about an accent to me when I asked you for details, but that's what BB told Cora Mae."

"What accent?" Marlin asked.

"He had an accent," BB said. "Like he came from someplace else."

"I didn't notice," Remy said. "I don't think so."

BB nodded. "From down south, or New Jersey, or . . ."

"What did it sound like?" I said, annoyed all over again by BB's lack of experience with regional dialects.

A look of comprehension crossed Marlin's face as BB fumbled through his version of the warden's accent. Marlin gave BB a light punch in the arm.

"That wasn't an accent, BB," he said.

"That was a stutter."

"Are you sure?" I said, remembering Warden Burnett's speech impediment.

"Dead sure," Marlin said.

I shuddered at the thought of a renegade warden. I could take on any local Joe the Man resident without a quiver in my hand or a moment's hesitation. I had a weapons purse filled with an arsenal of reinforcements like my trusty pepper spray and a cattle prod that could zap your socks off.

But a legally armed DNR agent with ties to the government was another matter.

What was Burnett doing out in the woods that day and what did it mean?

I didn't like the possibilities.

Nineteen

While I waited for Kitty and Cora Mae to finish at Billy's funeral, I leaned against the Lincoln, feeling the warmth of the sun on my face. I was trying to watch the road, watch Fred, and sort through a jumble of disconnected ideas involving Warden Burnett.

Fred sniffed around the vehicles in the parking lot and selected a Ford pickup with fancy rims. He lifted his leg on the tire. Taking his sweet time, he chose again and did the same thing on Dickey's Chevy. He seemed to like to spread his authority around.

I whistled after tire number three, and he ran over and jumped into the back seat. I glanced back at the road just in time to see the Mitch Movers truck roar past, heading south.

I didn't have time to blow the horn and wait for my partners to dawdle out. At the truck's missile-launching rate of speed as it zinged past, I'd have a tough time catching up.

The key was in the ignition, which saved me a second or two of precious time. I cranked the engine and almost ripped the gear shift off when I jammed it into drive.

The only thing I hadn't anticipated was that Kitty would have the seat pushed all the way back. I could barely reach the pedals, but I scrunched down, stretched out, and buried the pedal against the floorboard.

At times like this I really need Kitty and her NASCAR driving, but I'll deny ever saying it if I get through this chase in one piece. I'm a rookie and I've proven it with several dips into the ditch. My biggest mistake of all was when I rolled and totaled Barney's truck. But before that there was the mailbox disaster and the hole in my barn wall when I mistakenly thought I was in reverse.

Let's face it. I can't even pass a written driving test.

No way could I pull off the stunt Kitty had managed when she forced the van to stop the last time. Pulling alongside a moving vehicle and strong-arming it off the road is best performed by movie stuntmen and large, overly aggressive women.

A tiny speck in the distance reassured me

that I hadn't lost my target yet. I never let up on the gas, and the car's speed climbed steadily until the Lincoln's frame began to shake. I had to ease off or risk ripping the car apart.

I continued to gain while I tried to formulate a workable plan. The problem with impromptu car chases is the lack of a foolproof prearranged plan. I had to make it up as I went, and nothing was coming to mind.

I couldn't believe my good luck when the van crossed the four-way stop in Stonely and pulled into the Deer Horn Restaurant's parking lot. The driver strode into the restaurant as I pulled up behind him.

I ran to the van and peeked through the window into the driver's seat, but the tinted windows obscured my view. I glanced at the restaurant, then opened the driver's door and stuck my head inside. He hadn't left the truck running and he'd pulled the keys.

After pressing my ear against the van's side and hearing nothing, I marched into the Deer Horn. I'd have to think of some way to grab the keys away from him and steal the truck so I could discover what this important shipment contained.

Ruthie looked up from the counter. "Hi, Gertie," she said.

The driver, standing at the counter, turned and glanced at me. Then he did a double take. It was the same guy Kitty had run off the road in our overzealous hijacking attempt. The same one I'd zapped with my stun gun.

He frowned as if he was trying to remember where he'd seen me. If he placed me, I was in trouble.

"What can I get for you," Ruthie said to him, and he turned his attention back to her and away from me.

"A coffee and whatever sandwich you already have made up," he said, digging in a back pocket for his wallet. "To go."

No sign of the keys on the counter. They must be in his pocket.

"I'll see you later," I said to Ruthie, turning away so the driver couldn't study my face. I didn't want to refresh his memory. "I thought Carl might be in here."

"Haven't seen him," she replied, tallying the driver's bill.

"I'm leaving my dog out in the car. Will you check on him if he howls?"

"Sure," Ruthie said behind me, sounding puzzled.

By the time the driver returned to the truck and started off, I was lying in the back of the van where he wouldn't find me unless he threw open the back and dug around.

I couldn't believe I had the bravery, or stupidity, to pull off this stunt, but here I was, wedged between stacks of crates.

There wasn't a bird or an egg or a feather anywhere in the moving van. Granted, it was dark inside and I couldn't see very well, but I also couldn't smell anything, hear anything, or sense anything moving. Therefore, no birds.

I was disappointed.

The only explanation I could come up with was that they had two trucks that looked alike and they used the other one to transport the birds. I'd bummed a ride on the wrong van.

By the time I realized my mistake, we were gathering speed and leaving Stonely far behind us. But my eyes were adjusting to the darkness, and I peered at my surroundings.

All around me were piles of boxes. Long, wooden, coffin-like boxes stacked one on top of the other.

The van's shocks needed replacing. I felt every bump in the road. Whatever was inside the boxes rattled continuously. If I didn't go right to jail for this caper, I'd complain to the highway department about the condition of its roads.

I could see part of the back of the driver's head up front as he ate his sandwich and sipped coffee from a Styrofoam cup.

I really should find a way to inspect the boxes. A private investigator doesn't overlook any opportunity to check things out, even if they don't seem to pertain to the business at hand. But how was I going to open the boxes without the driver noticing? Better yet, how was I going to get back to the Deer Horn Restaurant to pick up Fred and Kitty's car?

What if our destination was Chicago or Detroit? I didn't have time for an extended vacation until after Little Donny was cleared of all charges and the real murderer was put away.

Easing the stun gun out of my purse, I crept along the top of the boxes until I was right behind the driver but still protected from view by a partition. I waited for my chance.

Ideally, I didn't want to zap him while he was barreling along at sixty-five miles an hour. No way could I wrestle for control of the wheel at a high speed. I really didn't have a death wish in spite of some of the situations I get myself into.

Although I knew this area of the country like the back of my liver-spotted hand, I'd said the same thing about the woods, and ended up walking in circles. This time I was sure of where we were. I'd traveled this stretch of road thousands of times on my way into Escanaba.

The van driver would soon come to a stop sign and make a right turn. That could be my last chance to take over until we arrived in the city, where we'd run into traffic and pedestrians and cops in squad cars. A little voice inside advised me against waiting too long.

I saw my opening looming ahead. Time slowed to a crawl as the moving van approached the stop sign. It took the driver forever to slow and finally stop.

His right turning signal clicked on.

Head check both ways just like in my instruction book.

In one fast motion, I turned on the stun gun and touched it to the back of his neck.

His body began to twitch and his hands flew from the steering wheel. His foot must have left the brake because the van started moving forward, edging through the stop.

I jumped through the opening into the front seat on top of him and grabbed the wheel, steering toward the side of the road while my foot floundered for the brake.

It was some task with his body in the way.

He reached out for my arm and I zapped him again as my foot found the brake and the van jerked to a halt a few yards off the road. I threw the gearshift into park.

Now what?

I couldn't drive with him hogging the driver's seat and me practically in the passenger seat. And he was far too heavy to move. I zapped him again for good measure and did the only thing I could do.

I reached across his limp body, opened the driver's door, and pushed him out. He rolled out face first and fell like a sack of Michigan potatoes.

There wasn't a car in sight when I pulled away and made a U-turn back toward Stonely. I looked in the side mirror and saw him stagger to his feet.

After a while when I had some distance between us, I turned onto a side road and parked on a soft shoulder along a line of tamaracks.

The boxes in the van were loosely sealed with a few nails. One of the wooden tops came away easily to expose a sheet of packing paper.

I grew nervous and stopped for a moment to consider the consequences of what I was about to do. There was no turning back now that I'd thrown the driver out and stolen his van.

If what was under the paper were blankets for the homeless shelter or teddy bears for a children's hospital, I'd have to start running for cover and stay there for the rest of my life. Blaze would jail me for sure.

I leaned back on my heels and took a big breath. Slowly I peeled away the layer of paper and peered inside.

Living in the U.P. makes you an expert on subjects that city folks don't even think about. For example, we know which leaves make the best toilet paper. We can tell the difference between a chipmunk and a squirrel, and we know that deer ticks are smaller than regular wood ticks. We also know our weapons. We know the difference between a gun and a rifle.

So I knew what I was looking at even though I'd only seen pictures.

Right before my eyes, shining in a brand-spanking-new sort of way, were cases and cases of Uzi-like machine guns.

Not toy guns like little tykes play shoot-'em-up with.

These were the real McCoy.

My best guess was that they were not registered and certainly illegal.

I thought about dumping the van in the

woods and running for the hills, just as I knew I'd have to if the boxes contained toys. If my grandson hadn't been in the middle of this mess, I might have done exactly that.

About now, I'd settle for a truck full of birds. Better yet, a nice game of four-cornered bingo with the seniors at the community center. Blaze's rage when he found out about the hijacked van seemed like a piece of rhubarb pie compared to what the owner of this shipment would feel when he found out his van was missing, along with all his machine guns. Ted Latvala and his band of thugs would be on my trail like a disturbed hive of angry bees on a dog's back.

No wonder the warden had been killed. He'd discovered the machine guns. And Little Donny had to be eliminated, too. He knew who did it.

Fingers of fear gripped my chest and squeezed until I reminded myself that Little Donny needed me to be strong. It was my most obvious and glaring characteristic, one some people have criticized me for. Tough as wood screws. Strong as plastic wrap. Or as Blaze likes to say, as unrelenting as mosquitoes at a picnic.

Calm down, I said to myself, encouragingly. This isn't so bad.

291

With any luck, the driver wouldn't remember what hit him or who threw him out of his truck. I tried to recall if I'd seen recognition in his eyes while we were going through the whole zapping thing, but I'd been busy steering and figuring out how to take his truck away.

Okay, here's my new revised plan, simple and guaranteed to work.

I'd drive back to the restaurant and pick up Fred. Then I'd turn the van over to Blaze and explain everything. Even if he didn't believe me he'd have to acknowledge a truck full of guns. Ted Latvala wouldn't have time for retribution. He wouldn't know what was coming his way until it was too late.

I was in the driver's seat again in more ways than one.

If this all worked out, along with giving up sugar doughnuts, I promised I'd also change my ways.

I'd take the driving test and start observing the law like everybody else.

I'd figure out a way to get along with Blaze and I'd spend more time in the kitchen working on recipes for my future cookbook.

If this all worked out, I'd stay out of trouble.

I promised.

TWENTY

Fred was helping Ruthie in the kitchen when I rushed in. He was checking the floor for cleanliness and lapping up any stray tidbits before they went to waste in Ruthie's dustpan.

"I thought he'd rather stay in here," she said. "He didn't like the car."

"The health inspector will close you down if he sees Fred in your kitchen," I warned.

"No one's around right now. Mondays are always slow. Besides, the howling going on outside would have drawn the fire department if all the volunteers weren't at the funeral. Fred sounds just like the siren they use to call in help when a fire breaks out."

I shook my head. "Anyone who has a house fire during hunting season or during a wedding or funeral is out of luck," I said. "Can I use your phone?"

"Help yourself."

Fred stuck his head in the garbage to

293

make sure Ruthie wasn't frivolously throwing away perfectly good food while I dialed Blaze's office.

Fred came up with several questionable items and gave them the taste test.

"Thanks for watching him. I owe you one," I said, when no one answered. I hustled Fred out to the van. He hopped into the passenger seat, his red eyes staring straight ahead in anticipation of our next journey. He thought this was all great fun.

Car rides, free food, new tires to explore. What could be better?

I started the motor but before I could pull out of the parking lot, a cell phone on the dashboard rang. Because I'm not one of those people who can drive and talk on a phone at the same time, I braked, picked it up, and read the incoming number illuminated on a tiny screen.

I didn't recognize the number.

It rang eight times. Then it stopped. I stared at it. Then it began to ring again.

If the driver didn't answer, would Latvala know something was wrong? Did they have a prearranged signal to warn them of trouble?

I studied the phone's keypad and wondered which button would turn the phone on. Heather and Star had cell phones but I never felt I needed one, so my knowledge was limited.

On the sixth ring, I figured it out and answered in the gruffest, lowest voice I could manage. "Yah," I said, briskly, holding the miniature phone to my ear.

"You've made a deadly mistake," a man said on the other end, slowly accentuating each syllable so I couldn't possibly misunderstand him.

I didn't know what to say, just continued to hold the phone to my ear. That turned out okay because he didn't care about a titillating two-way conversation.

"One word of this to anyone," he said, "and you can start planning a funeral for a loved one."

Continuing my best male imitation I said, "Are you threatening me?"

"No," he said. "I'm suggesting a trade. The van and all its contents for a life."

Trade? Who was he talking about? Cora Mae and Kitty were at the funeral. Little Donny and Blaze were killing time at the jail. If he had Grandma Johnson he would have let her go the minute she opened her mouth and started crabbing. Or he would have shot her on the spot.

He was bluffing.

"You're bluffing," I said.

"This is between me and you and no one else. Here's what you're going to do . . ."

I frowned in frustration because this wasn't working out exactly as planned. I had to maintain control. Who did he think he was, anyway? I had the power seat and I wasn't giving it up to some two-bit weapons dealer.

"You're all done dancing," I said, interrupting him, taking my stance. "You better turn yourself in. I'm taking the truck to the sheriff as we speak."

He laughed. "That's a good idea. I'll call you back." And he hung up.

Not only did I have the truck filled with machine guns as proof of an illegal gun ring, but I also knew the identity of the caller.

I dug in my weapons purse and pulled out my micro-recorder. After rewinding it, I punched the play button and listened to the tape I'd made the day I went to Marquette.

He'd tried to disguise his voice by speaking slowly, but I'd picked up on it in spite of his efforts.

The stutter.

I only had to listen to the tape for a few seconds to be sure.

The two voices, the one on my player and the one on the cell phone, were identical.

No question about it.

The caller was Warden Burnett.

I swung out of the parking lot and headed for the local jail, where I hoped to find Blaze.

Maybe Burnett and Latvala started out trafficking in illegal raptors. Then they moved to something more lucrative. Machine guns. An honest warden had stumbled on the scheme. Burnett tried to dissuade him in what he thought was a reasonable way. We'll count you in, he'd probably said. But Warden Hendricks took his job seriously. When Burnett realized that his efforts were wasted on Hendricks, he decided to kill him.

The idea came to him as they argued over Carl's doughnut heap.

Burnett saw Little Donny's rifle leaning against the tree and no one else at the bait pile.

A perfect opportunity. He didn't even have to use the gun in his holster.

What luck.

Except Little Donny popped out of his slumber chamber after the thunderous explosion, dodged a round of bullets, and escaped into the backwoods with the image of the killer seared in his memory.

Or so Burnett would have thought.

Burnett had been wearing coveralls over

his uniform. He chased after Little Donny just like my grandson described, taking Carl's bow and arrows along. But Little Donny had vanished.

When the Detroit boys encountered Burnett before the shooting, he was dressed in his brown uniform, so he must have changed into the coveralls after he passed their bail pile. His mind really wasn't on arresting the Smith brothers. He had another more important mission.

Afterwards, in his rush, he left the ATV on the side of the road rather than take the time to load it on his truck bed. He probably planned to pick it up later. He would have driven north, the direction he had seen Little Donny running.

And Burnett would have tried to head him off.

Maybe he waited in the deep woods for a long time before Billy Lundberg stumbled along wearing Little Donny's ball cap.

Burnett, relieved that the only witness had been eliminated, didn't find out until later that he'd murdered the wrong man.

Either he forgot the ATV or he thought it was risky to go back for it.

The only unexplained question involved the dead warden, Hendricks. How did he get to the bait pile if he wasn't with Burnett, and if his car was found in Marquette?

Everything else fit together perfectly.

And I had Burnett cold. I could wrap this case up in the next twenty minutes.

I took my foot off the brake and headed out.

At first I thought he was dead.

But when I rolled him over onto his back, he groaned.

His pulse was steady and strong but he had a lump on the back of his head the size of an ostrich egg.

I picked up the phone on the desk and called home. Heather answered.

"Blaze is hurt," I said. "Call an ambulance and come over to the jail. Bring Star for support if she's home."

"What's happened?" she asked.

"I don't have time to explain. Go in my closet. There's a shoe box on the floor. Inside you'll find Grandma's .38 revolver. There's a box of ammunition in my night-stand." I pulled Blaze's firearm from his holster. "I don't think he'll feel like chasing bad guys, but if he comes around and insists, he'll need a weapon."

Blaze's handgun felt heavy in my fist. It was a Glock. I always wanted one of these. Now I had one.

I looked at the empty jail cell where Little Donny had slept the night before.

Fred howled from the van.

Anyone else coming on this scene would jump to the wrong conclusion. They would think Little Donny had escaped after attacking his own uncle.

I grabbed the bedsheet from the cell cot and ran for the van.

"Now do you believe me?" Burnett said when he called back.

I was already on my way to Latvala's but I didn't want him to know that. If I was wrong about their location . . . well . . . I couldn't even imagine it.

"Where is he?" I demanded, abandoning the husky voice.

"Safe," he said. "For now."

"What do you want?"

"Weren't you listening? I want the van."

If he got the van, no way was he going to let Little Donny go free. Or me, for that matter. Little Donny might already be dead.

"I want to speak with him," I said in a tone of voice that I hoped commanded attention.

He hesitated and my heart skipped a beat.

I heard murmuring in the background, then Little Donny came on the line. I jammed a knuckle in my mouth to keep from crying.

"I'm okay," he said. "All he wants is the van and then he'll let me go."

He. He would have said *they* if more than one person was guarding him at the moment. Little Donny was alone with the warden.

"Where are you?"

But he was gone from the phone.

"You have twenty minutes to meet me," Burnett said. "And come alone. If I see anyone else, he dies."

"Where?"

He gave me directions to an isolated stretch of gravel road between Stonely and Marquette. I had to have more time.

"I need an hour."

"No way."

"I need to stop for gas and —"

"Thirty minutes." He hung up.

I had a slight advantage because I knew who he was. He wouldn't count on that.

What was Burnett doing to Little Donny right now? If I was a black-hearted killer, what would my next move be?

I'd finish off Little Donny now that his grandmother knew he was alive, and I'd ambush the van in a desolate area where no one would stumble along and witness my next move — which would be to kill its driver.

I had no intention of meeting Burnett on his terms. Crevice Road was my target, and I had to get there fast before he could carry out his plan to harm Little Donny and leave there to meet me.

The funeral home appeared in view ahead of me. I must have been traveling at a hundred miles an hour when I blew by. Cora Mae, Kitty, and Grandma were out in the parking lot, wandering around, searching for Kitty's car. Other mourners were filing out of the building, shaking hands and hugging each other.

I wanted to stop and pick up Cora Mae and Kitty but I couldn't spare an extra second. Besides, I couldn't deal with Grandma Johnson right now.

Kitty glanced up at the moving van streaking past and her mouth dropped open and stayed there. She couldn't see me through the tinted windows so she had to assume I was one of "them."

I hate my old lady reflexes.

By the time I found the automatic window control, slid it down, and called out to them, we had passed into Maple County, and the only one who heard my cry for help

was my buddy, Fred.
  He stretched and kissed my face.

Twenty-One

We soared over the ruts at such speed that we didn't even feel the bumps and bangs. If I pulled the entire transmission off the van, I didn't care as long as I got there before anything bad happened.

"Smell this," I said to Fred, rubbing the bed sheet against his nose. He knew the drill. Fred sniffed and snorted even more when I attached his leash, a tricky maneuver while keeping a watchful eye on the road, but I've always been a multitasker. What woman isn't?

Ted Latvala's house loomed directly ahead. My palms on the steering wheel felt sweaty. I glanced at the Glock resting between my legs. I eased the safety off.

Joe the Man lived close enough to Latvala to offer support — if he was sober — but I couldn't risk a moment's delay. I had visions of a revolver slowly rising in a cold, steady hand and a grimace on my grandson's face as he squeezed his eyes shut and waited for the end.

I shook the image off.

The plan was simple and ill-prepared, as all my plans were. I'd drive in slowly like I belonged there. Unless someone came right up to the van, I wouldn't be recognized.

I'd do anything to get Little Donny back in one piece, even if it meant shooting a gaping hole right through the windshield and picking off every single one of them.

All those years of target practice were about to pay off. At the beginning I'd crabbed and complained that the family should take up a more meaningful hobby, but they'd voted me down. Every Sunday afternoon when the kids were small, we'd have "family time" with weapons slung over our shoulders and a box of ammo at our feet. BB guns, pellet guns, and tin cans at first. After that, as the kids grew, we graduated to shotguns and pistols.

Fred began to make whimpering noises, licking his lips and working himself up for the hunt. His entire hundred-pound mass, seated patiently on the passenger seat during most of the drive, heaved into a standing position as though he could sense that we were near our destination.

I was about to see him in action.

I forced my foot onto the brake and slowed for the turn into the weapon-making camp. I'd only attract unwanted attention if I barreled in at seventy miles an hour with two wheels off the gravel.

We crept past the side of the house without seeing anyone. A light was on in the welding workshop and the large building's bay doors were open, so I cautiously pulled in next to another, identical moving van, ready for trouble.

No one was there.

I hopped out and opened the other van. The smell hit me first. It was loaded with feathers and bird droppings. Illegal bird sales and gun trafficking. What an operation. They truly believed in diversification.

I wound the end of Fred's leash around my wrist. I didn't have to coax him out of the van, but when I started in the direction of the workshop, he locked his legs and resisted.

I tried pulling the lug. He wouldn't budge. I looped the leash around the top post of a wooden fence running next to the building and hoped he wouldn't start howling. As long as he had me in his sights, I thought he'd stay quiet.

Crouching down, I ran for the back of the workshop and peered in, careful not to

306

touch the windows that were wired to set off an alarm.

Ted Latvala, wearing safety goggles, worked on something at a table. Sparks flew. Faintly, I could hear country and western music playing from a radio on a shelf above his head.

Little Donny wasn't inside.

Latvala began to whistle along with the tune on the radio. Either he didn't know that his partner in crime was systematically picking off witnesses or he didn't care.

A bolt of fear shot through me. What if Little Donny wasn't even on the property?

Don't think that.

Maybe they had him in the house. I ran back to Fred and turned toward the house. He wouldn't budge.

Then I realized why. Fred was supposed to tell me where Little Donny was, not the other way around. If my canine partner insisted that Little Donny wasn't in the house, that was that. I had to trust him.

I put the safety back on the Glock because I knew what I was in for if Fred picked up a scent. I didn't want to accidentally shoot either one of us.

"Okay, Fred," I whispered, clutching the leash. "Tell me where he is."

At first, Fred didn't move. Then he sniffed

the ground. Slowly, he made his way back into the building housing the vehicles. Back out again.

"Please, Fred," I said, softly. "Find a trail."

He worked his way around to the back of the building, taking his time, checking out every little patch of ground. I saw the expression on his face change. His body became rigid and he began to move.

Fred dragged me toward the woods at a fast clip and headed down a deer trail. The way we were thrashing through the pines and hardwoods I knew one of two things would happen soon. Either Fred would sweep me off my feet and pull me along on the ground until I lost my end of the leash, or Burnett would hear us coming a mile away and set up an ambush.

The crazed dog dug in his hind legs and strained ahead like one of the local sled dogs during our annual mid-distance race. I wouldn't have had much luck controlling him even if his weight didn't hover close to mine. Beefy No-Neck hadn't done much better at handling him.

Fred swept me off my feet just like I'd feared and I crashed to the ground, skimming through last season's layer of dried leaves and a few of this year's. Fred paused when he started pulling my additional weight and looked back. We slowed and he gave me a moment to regain my footing. Then we were off again.

Where several deer paths merged, Fred lost the trail. He ran in circles while I got my bearings and caught my breath. I could tell when he found it again because his ears straightened up and his head swung eagerly toward a trail to our left.

By then I had his leash wound around a young maple. "Sorry, Fred," I whispered. "But you have to wait here. Your enthusiasm will get us killed."

The howling started as soon as I disappeared out of sight and a minute later I heard a voice ahead.

"What's that?" I heard Little Donny say. "Wolves?"

I sidled up behind an old oak tree and saw Warden Burnett sitting on an ATV, a revolver loose in his hand. "Shut up and finish," he said. "I have to go meet your granny and I don't want to keep her waiting."

Little Donny stood in a shallow hole, holding a shovel. He wiped his face with the back of his hand and left a streak of dirt across his cheek. He looked scared.

Burnett had watched too many crime movies. He was making my grandson dig his own grave.

I should plug him right between the eyes for that. I was a little worried about the distance between us but I couldn't get closer without exposing myself. I'd take the best shot I could from here.

Another howl.

"It sounds like a whole pack of them," Little Donny said, pale and nervous.

"Lay down. Let's see if you fit."

I eased off the safety on my favorite new handgun and wished I'd had time to shoot a few practice rounds.

The rubbing of the metal when the safety released sounded like an explosion to me, but Burnett didn't turn his head.

Before Little Donny could comply, the crashing of a large animal resounded through the forest. Another howl, closer this time, as branches broke and leaves crunched.

"What if it's a bear?" Little Donny said.

"Bears don't howl," Burnett answered, starting to look worried.

I felt the displacement of air as Fred swooshed past me, the leash bouncing behind him.

Burnett glanced up in shock and saw a black wild animal descending on him. He lifted his weapon and took aim.

I pulled the trigger of my Glock.

And heard another shot almost simultaneously. Burnett had fired at Fred.

Fred seemed to hesitate, although he didn't drop. He continued running forward, his legs pumping much slower now, easing off, winding down.

I screamed and ran from the protection of the tree. Little Donny put his arms out in front of him as though warding off an attack.

Then Burnett grimaced, dropped his gun, and fell off the ATV backwards.

Fred pounced on Little Donny, driving him backwards, and grabbed a firm hold on his pants.

Burnett groaned and clutched his knee. I kicked his revolver away, picked it up, and bent over to admire my handiwork. Not exactly a bull's eye, but close. With any luck, his kneecap was shattered.

Since Little Donny was indisposed and it looked like Fred would live, I took the opportunity to hit Burnett in the back with the shovel. Then I commanded Fred to release my grandson and hugged Little Donny, ignoring the tears pooling in his eyes.

Then I checked Fred for gaping bullet holes.

He was absolutely fine.

I wondered if all those wardens running around in the woods with firearms were required to prove they could shoot straight before they started pointing them at local residents.

What a lousy aim.

"That's the guy," Little Donny said, pointing at Burnett. "I saw what he did at our bait pile. And he hit Uncle Blaze in the head with his gun."

"Blaze is going to be okay," I said. "Did he see that it was Burnett who conked him?"

Little Donny shook his head. "Blaze was asleep at his desk. He didn't know what hit him."

Stands to reason, I thought. The man should retire before he gets himself killed.

I noticed Burnett was making all kinds of faces as he rolled around on the ground. That had to hurt.

"Let's go," I said. "We'll send somebody back for him."

Little Donny wanted to tie him up with Fred's leash. "How will he hold his knee if we bind his hands," I reasoned, suddenly hit with a blast of compassion. "We'll get you help," I told Burnett, but I wasn't sure he heard me.

Little Donny hopped in the driver's seat

of the ATV and we rode back slowly, with Fred running loose alongside the machine.

Stopping right before the tree line and cutting the engine, we discussed strategy.

"I'm not leaving without the van," I said.

"We should drive the ATV to a neighbor's house and call for help," Little Donny said. "There's another guy around here somewhere."

"If you mean a really hairy guy, he's in the workshop."

"That's him."

"He isn't paying any attention." The trusty Glock and my most recent display of hot shooting accounted for most of my inflated bravado. Having a strapping big grandson and a devil dog at my side also helped.

Bring 'em on.

TWENTY-TWO

The van wouldn't start.

"I hate it when things go wrong," I said, turning the key again.

Nothing. Total silence. Not even a sputter or grinding noise.

We sat in the van inside the building and stared at the ignition.

"Let's get out of here," Little Donny said. "We can walk out and come back with support."

"What if they move the van and we lose our evidence?"

"We still have Burnett cold."

"I want it all," I said. Before the day was through, I planned on nabbing the entire gun and bird ring. Right now, there was no way of knowing if any of the others were accessories to the murders. Every last one of them was going down. Burnett, Latvala, the driver I'd zapped, and any other stragglers we could round up.

Then the alarm went off, the same piercing alert that I'd set off when I touched the workshop window. Did Latvala know we were in the building and hit the alarm to call in reinforcements? Or had someone else triggered it?

I shook my head. "This wasn't part of the plan," I muttered.

Little Donny turned to open his door.

"Stay here with Fred," I said. "Don't move from this van no matter what happens."

I dashed to the edge of the open garage bay and peeked out toward the noise. I saw Kitty and Cora Mae scrambling for cover. Dickey's deputy truck idled in the driveway with Grandma Johnson sitting in the passenger seat. Her head barely cleared the bottom of the windshield, but I saw those snarly eyes.

Kitty must have taken Dickey's truck to chase the moving van and blundered in without thinking it through. The pin-curled wonder should learn to look before she leaps. I should know.

Now we all were in a pickle.

The alarm abruptly stopped and Latvala stormed out with his rifle.

I was too far away to get a shot. All I'd manage to do if I fired was announce my position.

Kitty and Cora Mae screeched in unison when they tore open the bird shed door to hide inside and felt falcon wings beating at them. Cora Mae had her hands over her hair and both of them ducked down before turning and running toward the house, leaving the coop door open.

Birds started flying out. Some of the young ones had probably never flown free before. Birds of all sizes continued to stream out and take to the air. Diving, dipping, circling, most of them coming to rest behind the coop in a towering maple. A few made for the trees along the woods and perched atop the pines.

Cora Mae and Kitty must have thought they had landed in Hitchcock's classic thriller, *The Birds,* because they were making more racket than the confused raptors.

The screen door slammed and they were inside the house.

Latvala loped to the bird coop, realized he was too late to stop the birds, turned sharply, and ran back to the driveway. He spotted Grandma Johnson.

She took one look at the hairy man with the rifle, lunged over to the driver's seat, and ripped backwards into the road. She continued in reverse so long I thought she'd never find the brake or the correct gear. The

316

truck jerked to a halt, then it took off down the road, heading toward Stonely. Latvala ran down the drive, fired at her, and a side window blew out.

I almost dropped my Glock. Since when did she know how to drive?

A cell phone rang.

Latvala reached in his pocket and answered it. As he came closer, I could hear part of his conversation.

I heard him say, "This has gotten out of hand, Burnett." He walked back up the driveway, looking for his next escaped quarry. "You're on your own."

His eyes scanned the treetop. A zillion night hunters' eyes followed him.

Rats. I forgot about Burnett's cell phone.

"You want me to shoot all of them?" Latvala said in disbelief. "How many are here, anyway? Some old midget just got away. I'm telling you, I'm clearing out. I think they're even in the house."

He listened for a moment.

"This isn't the first time I've had to relocate. I can do it again. Latvala, Jones, Wazinski. I'm due for a new name. At least the shipment went out. I'm picking up the money and disappearing."

Another pause while he listened.

"Don't threaten me," he said. "Sure I

dropped him off in the woods and I roughed him up a little to get the message across, but you killed him. I'm outta here."

He closed the phone and returned it to his pocket. It rang again but he ignored it.

Sirens wailed in the distance as Latvala ran for a truck parked in the driveway. Before I could chase him, I saw Kitty bolt out of the house with Cora Mae trailing.

"Drop the rifle," Kitty shouted from the side of the house. She held a machine gun in front of her. Kitty looked exactly like a wanted poster.

Latvala took one look and dropped the rifle.

Cora Mae appeared from a hiding spot behind Kitty and sashayed over, dangling her handcuffs from an index finger. She'd found more uses for those things . . .

"It's over," I called to Little Donny. "You can come out now."

The sirens grew louder and two state troopers pulled into the driveway. By then, Kitty had chucked the machine gun in case the cops thought she was the perp.

Little Donny, Cora Mae, Kitty, Fred, and I formed a circle around Latvala, who sat on the gravel with his hands cuffed behind his back.

"I called nine-one-one from the house," Cora Mae said. "They sure got here fast."

"Hey, Johnny G.," Kitty called, recognizing one of the officers. "Have I got a story for you!" She lumbered over to the squad car and bent over the open window, exposing the back of her legs clear up to her panty line.

"I'll go talk to them, too," Little Donny said.

"Help!" Latvala called out. "They're holding me against my will."

I kicked him in the shin. "Shut up," I said. "You'll get your turn to talk, but you're last on the agenda."

"How did you get here?" Cora Mae asked me while Kitty and Little Donny told their version of the story to the cops.

"I was driving the van," I said.

"I didn't know that," Cora Mae shrieked. "We wanted to follow it but couldn't find our car. Kitty looked in Dickey's truck and can you believe it, he left his keys in the ignition? What kind of police officer would do that?"

"One that doesn't know Kitty," I replied.

"We saw it turn onto Crevice Road but then we lost it, and we ended up at the house down the road."

"Joe the Man."

"Exactly," Cora Mae shrieked again. "How did you know?"

"I met him."

"I had to sit on his lap before he'd tell us about the neighbors. That's what held us up."

"What you'll do for your job, Cora Mae." She beamed.

Another squad car pulled into the driveway and I could see Grandma Johnson in the back. All that was visible was the top of her hat.

The officers got out of their cars.

"They weren't responding to our call," Kitty said to Cora Mae. She glanced at me. "Dickey reported his truck stolen and the state troopers were combing the area."

One of the officers piped up. "We apprehended the car thief at the end of the road," he said. "I had to handcuff her. She actually tried to resist arrest." He rubbed his shoulder. "She must have rocks in that purse."

I covered my mouth to keep from laughing.

"She said she witnessed a shootout. Since one of the truck windows was missing, we thought there might be something to her story."

"Someone that age . . ." another officer

began. "You'd think she'd be home knitting."

"No driver's license either," the first officer said.

"Runs in the family," Cora Mae said.

TWENTY-THREE

"Blaze helped round them up," I said to Cora Mae and Kitty after speaking to him on the phone. "They arrested three others besides Latvala and Burnett." Little Donny and Heather sat at the kitchen table with us, eating leftover pasties. Little Donny's pasty was drowning in a pool of ketchup.

"Blaze is okay then?" Kitty asked.

"He wouldn't let the ambulance take him to the hospital," Heather said.

"He always was a hard-head," I agreed. "He never gives up. Now he wants to take my fingerprints again because the first set was inconclusive. The case is over, I told him. Forget it."

"What will happen to all the falcons?" Cora Mae asked.

"I called the wildlife rehabilitation center," I said. "They sent someone over to try to round them up and help the birds acclimate to the wild. At the very least, they'll feed them until they learn to hunt."

Fred sprawled next to the table. Kitty saw me looking down at him.

"We heard the ululating coming from the woods, didn't we, Cora Mae? And we knew it was Fred."

"He's quite the behemoth," I said, taking up the challenge.

"I signed up for that online law school," Kitty said. "I start next week."

"Good for you. Now the Trouble Busters have their own legal counsel."

Little Donny got up and returned from the cupboard with a bag of sugar doughnuts. We all dug in. Mine was halfway to my mouth when I remembered my promise to give them up if things worked out all right.

I looked around the table at my friends and family and realized how incredibly lucky I was. Not only that, my life was about to get even richer. George would be over later to help me study. That was one promise I planned on keeping, passing the driving test.

I bit into the doughnut.

The thought of George sitting next to me, just the two of us, alone, heads bent over the instruction manual, made me feel warm and fuzzy all over. Maybe it was time to consider taking the next step forward in our relationship.

Life couldn't be better.

Just then Grandma Johnson shuffled down the hall.

"What's this?" she demanded. "Some kind of party and I wasn't invited, as usual?"

"Anything exciting happen today?" I asked her.

"If you want to call attending a funeral for a drunken fool exciting, you go right ahead."

"Aren't you going to tell us about your arrest? Blaze said he almost couldn't get you released."

"And it's all your fault," Grandma said. "Running around with —" She stopped because she realized that the friends she was about to disparage were sitting right at the table. Grandma looked down. "With that big ugly mutt. I'm putting my foot down. It's either him or me, and that's that. And I'm telling you another thing . . ."

The kitchen cleared out quickly after that and I was left standing there alone while Grandma Johnson gave me an earful. Even Fred slunk out when I wasn't looking.

A few minutes later I heard Little Donny screaming from the garage. "What happened to my car?" he shouted.

I ran for cover.

RECIPES

North Woods Pasties

There's quite a debate over how pasties (pronounced pass-tees) came to the Upper Peninsula. Some say they arrived with the Cornish coal miners, who ate them for lunch deep underground. Others believe they originated with the Finns or Swedes. I stay out of the middle of it and just enjoy them.

This hearty dish can be found in little shops scattered throughout the U.P. The senior citizens in Stonely make the best I've ever had, and after a lot of experimenting, I think I've figured it out. They freeze well, so make a bunch. Serve with a pat of butter, or ketchup, or use your imagination.

Makes 6

For pastry:

3 1/2 cups all-purpose flour

1 tsp salt
1 cup butter, cut in pieces
3/4 cup ice water
1 egg

For filling:

1 pound coarse ground round
1 pound coarse ground pork
1 1/2 cups onions, chopped
1 cup rutabaga, diced
1 cup potatoes, diced
1 teaspoon salt
1/2 teaspoon pepper
1 tablespoon oil

Preheat oven to 400 degrees F.

Sift 3 cups flour and salt. Cut in butter until coarse like breadcrumbs. Slowly add ice water until the dough can be formed into a ball, wrap in plastic, and refrigerate for 20 minutes. In large bowl combine all filling ingredients. Grease baking sheet. Dust workspace with remaining flour, divide dough in 6 pieces and roll each into a circle the size of a plate. On half of each pasty, spread 1 cup of filling. Fold over and crimp edges. Place on baking sheet, cut a few slits in each top, brush with egg white, and bake 1 hour.

Grandma Johnson's Spam Casserole

I know Spam isn't on everyone's shopping list, and you're probably snickering right now. But we actually grew up eating the stuff. The old-timers did what they had to do to survive. Here's Grandma Johnson's county fair award winner. If you've never eaten Spam before, this is the way to start out.

2 cups macaroni noodles, cooked
1/2 pound cheddar cheese, cubed
2 tablespoons onion, chopped
2 tablespoons green pepper, chopped
1 can Spam, cubed
1 can cream of mushroom soup
1 cup canned peas
3/4 cup milk

Preheat oven to 350 degrees F. Combine all ingredients and bake for 30 minutes.

Caramel Apple Pie

In the early fall, the apple trees droop with the weight of hundreds of firm, ripe apples. That's when we get out our paper bags and fill them to the brim. Cortlands are my favorite, nice and tart. Try mixing and matching when you make your pies. Cortland, McIntosh, and Jonathan make a tangy,

spicy combination that's perfect for pie.
  Makes 1 pie

Buy 9-inch pie crust or make it with the following:

2 cups flour
1 teaspoon salt
3/4 cup shortening
5 tablespoons cold water

For pie filling:

3 tablespoons flour
1/2 cup sugar
1 teaspoon cinnamon
1/8 teaspoon salt
6 cups apples, peeled and sliced thin

For topping:

1 cup light brown sugar
1/2 cup flour
1/2 cup quick oatmeal
1 stick butter

Final touches:

1/2 cup pecans, chopped
caramel ice cream topping

Preheat oven to 325 degrees F and toast pecans on baking sheet for 5 minutes, or until brown, checking and turning often. Put aside for final touches.

Raise oven heat to 375 degrees F and make the crust if you haven't bought one. Combine flour and salt. Cut in shortening until crumbly and pea-sized. Sprinkle with cold water. Roll out on floured surface and line 9-inch pan.

Prepare filling. Stir all ingredients for pie filling together except apples. When mixed, add apples and gently fold in. Place in pie pan.

Prepare topping. Combine dry topping ingredients. Cut in butter until crumbly. Sprinkle on pie.

Line edges of piecrust with foil. Bake 25 minutes. Remove foil. Bake 30 more minutes or until brown. Remove from oven. Sprinkle with toasted pecans and drizzle caramel topping over.

ABOUT THE AUTHOR

Deb Baker grew up in the Michigan Upper Peninsula with the Finns and Swedes portrayed in *Murder Grins and Bears It.* She has an intimate knowledge of the life and people of the region.

She lives in North Lake, Wisconsin, with her husband, two teenagers, two dogs, and two cats. She is working on her third Yooper mystery, *Murder Talks Turkey.*

Deb is a member of Sisters in Crime, Mystery Writers of America, and the International Sled Dog Association, where she actively races sled dogs. Her short stories have appeared in numerous literary journals, including *Passages North* and *Room of One's Own.*

Visit Deb at www.debbakerbooks.com.

The employees of Thorndike Press hope you have enjoyed this Large Print book. All our Thorndike and Wheeler Large Print titles are designed for easy reading, and all our books are made to last. Other Thorndike Press Large Print books are available at your library, through selected bookstores, or directly from us.

For information about titles, please call:
   (800) 223-1244

or visit our Web site at:
   www.gale.com/thorndike
   www.gale.com/wheeler

To share your comments, please write:
   Publisher
   Thorndike Press
   295 Kennedy Memorial Drive
   Waterville, ME 04901